Vampire Diaries

UNSPOKEN

CHAPTER

1

Meredith desperately struggled against the metal restraints binding her arms and legs to the operating table. She closed her eyes, straining her muscles, adrenalin surging through her, but the restraints wouldn't budge.

'Please,' she begged, hot tears running down her cheeks.

Jack ignored her pleas, focusing intently on her neck as he slowly slid a hypodermic needle beneath her skin.

'Almost done,' he said, depressing the plunger. Meredith's neck was too numb to feel the needle, but the injection burned as it spread through her veins. She gasped and tried once more to rip her arm away from her captor.

Jack's eyes were on hers as she writhed. The same

warm hazel eyes as they'd been when Meredith had thought of him as a mentor, as one of the best hunters she'd ever met. Before she knew Jack was a vampire. Before he had murdered Stefan.

Before she'd known he was changing her.

'I don't want to be a vampire,' she whispered, her voice shaking. Her eyes blurred with tears. Meredith thought of Cristian, the vampire brother she'd had to kill, of the generations of her family whose life mission had been to destroy the supernatural race. She couldn't become one of the enemy, not after everything she'd been through.

A brief smile crossed Jack's face, the corners of his eyes crinkling. 'It's done.'

Meredith ached everywhere. She began to shake her head slowly, back and forth, as her breath came in ragged, anxious spurts. 'I'll kill myself,' she said desperately.

Jack grinned more widely. 'Go ahead and try,' he said. 'I've perfected the treatments. We're unkillable.'

With a fresh flare of panic, Meredith again slammed her arms and legs against the restraints. The heavy, numb feeling was fading, and metal bit sharply into her wrists. In a burst of effort, she snapped the metal bands, and was free. Meredith tumbled off the operating table and, still shaky on her feet, hit the floor hard.

On her hands and knees, she scrabbled for the door, expecting Jack to hoist her back on to the table at any moment. But Jack didn't make a move towards her, just watched as she struggled. She could hear herself breathing, a harsh, desperate panting, as she pulled herself across the floor. She just needed to get out.

She made it to the door and pulled herself up, hanging on to the knob.

'You'll be back,' Jack said, his voice an eerie calm.

Wrenching the door open, Meredith burst through and ran as fast as she could, stumbling through the hall. It was long and fluorescent-lit, the floors dark-grey tile like those of a hospital or a school. She listened for Jack's footsteps in the hall behind her, but there was only his laughter, bubbling maniacally, from the room she had left behind.

'You'll be back,' he called again. 'You won't be able to help it.'

Not letting herself think of anything but escape, Meredith looked around frantically. Double doors at the end of the hall led towards a stairway, and she pushed through, her feet slapping at the concrete stairs, heading down and – she hoped – out.

The stairs seemed to go on for ever. Finally, she burst through another set of double doors and on to the sidewalk. She paused for a moment, gasping for breath as she gazed around. Office buildings stretched behind her. She had no idea where she was. It was still dark out, but the sky was beginning to lighten towards grey.

Everything in her was screaming, *get away*, her heart

still hammering in panic. What if Jack's fierce, invulnerable vampires were nearby? Meredith pressed her back against the cold brick wall of the building behind her, trying to conceal herself in the darkness, and looked around cautiously. No one.

She sucked in a deep breath, trying to calm her pounding heart. There'd be no sense in running at random. She clenched her fists and deliberately relaxed, forcing the tension out of her body. She was steadier on her feet now, her arms and legs tingling as the numbness wore off. There was no one in sight. To her left, Meredith heard the sound of cars racing past on a highway. She headed in that direction, ready to find her way home.

Dawn was breaking as Meredith opened the door to her apartment and walked quietly through the entryway, dropping her keys on the table. *I'm all right now*, she told herself. Jack had said she was a vampire, but Meredith didn't feel any different. Maybe the treatment didn't take.

She took a deep breath as she glanced around her familiar bedroom. Early morning light was beginning to come through the curtained windows, and everything seemed comfortingly ordinary. Her law books were lined up on the shelf across from the bed, her and Alaric's wedding picture stood on top of her bureau. Without even bothering to take off her clothes, Meredith pulled back the cool sheets and slipped into bed. Next to her, Alaric muttered something in his sleep and burrowed deeper into the pillows.

She was safe. Everything was terrible: Stefan was dead, Jack was a vampire, but the worst hadn't happened. *I'm fine*, she told herself.

Experimentally, she ran a finger across her teeth. Normal. No extra-sharp canines. Her hands were warm, her heart was beating at a quick, human rate. She was fine. Her body must have fought off whatever Jack had tried to do.

She shifted closer to Alaric, then frowned. There was something in her jeans pocket. She reached inside and her fingers closed around a thin cardboard rectangle. A business card. Meredith squinted as she pulled it out and held it up to catch the dim morning light. Printed on the card was an infinity symbol in black type and a company name: *Lifetime Solutions*. Below that, handwritten in black ink, a phone number.

Jack had been pretty sure of himself, she thought angrily. She tightened her fingers around the card, crumpling it a little, before shoving it into the drawer of her bedside table. She didn't ever want to see Jack again.

According to her clock, it wasn't even five AM yet. Meredith took another deep breath and closed her eyes, trying to relax into sleep, trying to forget Jack's face as he slid the final needle into her arm.

Her bed was soft and the sheets smelled faintly of

detergent. There was another smell, too. Something . . . salty. Slightly metallic. Meredith frowned a little, trying to identify it.

Gradually, she became aware of a sound as well. All around her came a slow, regular rushing that reminded her of the ocean, a deep, slow thudding beneath the steady sound of the surf. Breathing in time with the sounds, Meredith sank deeper into almost-sleep.

Something kept tugging at the edges of her attention, though, sharpening her appetite. Without conscious intent, she licked her lips. That salty, metallic smell . . . there was something about it more delicious than the roasted chicken her mother made, sweeter than fresh-baked apple pie. So familiar, somehow, and yet she couldn't quite place it.

Meredith's mouth was watering hungrily when something suddenly shifted in her jaw. In surprise, her hands flew to her mouth.

Her jaw moved again. Tentatively, she touched her lips. They were so sensitive, she winced at the pain-pleasure when her careful fingers met her teeth. More cautiously, she touched again.

Her canines were long and sharp. Fangs.

The rushing, thudding sound, the smell of salt and something else – copper – was almost overwhelming. With each thud, her stomach ached and her teeth ached.

It was Alaric. She was hearing Alaric's heart beating.

She was smelling Alaric's blood.

Horrified, Meredith scrambled out of bed. She stared down at Alaric below her, so peaceful and oblivious.

Jack had done it. He'd turned her into a vampire.

And she was famished.

CHAPTER

2

*D*ear Diary,

I've lost everything. I've lost myself.

I don't know who I am without Stefan.

For days now, I haven't been able to write in here. I felt like, if I wrote down everything that's happened, it would make it real.

But it is real, whether I write it down or not.

Stefan is dead.

Elena pulled her hands away from her laptop as if it had burned her, then pressed her fingers tightly against her mouth. Stefan was dead. Her eyes filled with hot tears, and she roughly wiped them away. All she'd done lately was cry, and it wasn't making anything better.

It seems like the earth should have stopped turning. If

Stefan is dead, the sun shouldn't rise in the morning. But time passes and every day, there's a new day. Except it means nothing to me, because Stefan is still dead.

We all trusted Jack. He and Stefan hunted side by side, tracking down the Old One, Solomon. But while we were all celebrating Solomon's defeat, feeling happy and safe at last, Jack plunged his stave through Stefan's heart. Jack killed him.

Elena stopped typing again, and rested her head in her hands, remembering. Stefan's eyes had met Elena's and he'd given her a soft smile. She'd known that they were both thinking the same thing: *Now that the Old Ones are gone, our real life together can begin.*

It had all happened so fast. Elena had seen that something was wrong, but before she could shout a warning, Jack had thrust his stave through Stefan's heart. She'd been too late.

The smile had faded from Stefan's face as his eyes widened. For just a moment, he'd looked innocently surprised, and then Stefan had simply gone blank. His eyes – those leaf-green eyes that had looked at her with such love – lost focus. His body crumpled to the floor, but Stefan was already gone.

It was true that Jack was hunting the Old Ones, just as we were. But he didn't want to make the world safer. Jack had created a new kind of vampire through drugs and surgeries instead of blood and magic. The vampires Jack made are terrifying: immune to sunlight and vervain and, according to

Damon, impossible to kill by any of the usual methods.

Jack didn't want any competition for his lab-created race of vampires. So he set out to eliminate the most dangerous vampires, the oldest ones. Not just the ancient Old Ones, but also the clever, long-lived vampires who have lasted a few centuries. Vampires like Katherine and Damon. Like Stefan.

Jack used us all – my Guardian Power, Stefan and Meredith's fighting ability, Bonnie's magic – as weapons against Solomon. The Old One was too well hidden for Jack to find on his own. But once Solomon was dead, Stefan was just another obstacle in Jack's way.

We don't know where Jack is now, or what he's planning next. The hunters who travelled with him – Trinity, Darlene, and Alex – were as fooled by him as we were. They've left town, trying to track Jack. But they haven't got a clue where he might be.

Elena swallowed hard and wiped her eyes again with the sleeve of her bathrobe.

Meredith and Damon don't think Jack's really gone at all. A few days ago, Meredith fought one of his strange synthetic vampires. The vampire escaped and Meredith barely survived. Is Jack continuing his experiments here in Dalcrest?

I should care. I should want vengeance. But instead, I'm numb.

Without Stefan, it's like I'm dead, too.

A key rattled in the lock of the front door, and Elena looked up from her computer screen to see Damon coming in. The cold apartment warmed a bit, as if the sleek, dark-haired vampire had brought some of the late summer breeze into the air-conditioned room. He seemed to get smaller as he came in, though, hunching his shoulders. Through the bond between them, Elena sensed his wistful ache at finding himself once again surrounded by Stefan's possessions, resenting the reminder that his brother was gone.

'You've been feeding,' she commented, looking at the near-human flush of his cheeks.

'If you want to call it that.' Damon curled his lip in disgust. 'Stefan's animal diet is utterly vile, just as I always suspected.'

Elena flinched, and Damon glanced up, his face falling. 'I'm sorry,' he said. 'I know I shouldn't—' She could see her own pain at the mention of Stefan reflected in his eyes.

'It's OK,' she said, shaking her head hard. 'You should be able to say his name, he's your brother. I just—' Tears were rising up in her eyes again, and she willed them back. She needed to stop crying.

Damon took her hand, his fingers cool and smooth. 'I promise you that Jack will pay,' he said quietly, his eyes as dark as night. 'Whatever it takes.'

A wave of panic hit Elena, knocking the breath out of her, and she clutched Damon's hand between hers. 'No,' she said. 'Damon, you have to be careful. Even if it means letting Jack go.'

Damon stiffened, his dark eyes fixed on hers. 'We promised each other we would take vengeance on Jack,' he said firmly. 'We owe it to Stefan.'

Elena shook her head. 'I can't lose you, too.' She hated the weak waver in her voice, but she straightened her shoulders and looked at Damon levelly, her face resolute. Sometimes it felt like Damon's presence was the thin barrier between her and madness. Damon was the only one who understood, who'd really loved Stefan as deeply as she had.

Every night, she heard Damon's soft footfalls pacing through the apartment, living room to kitchen to hall, hesitating sometimes outside her bedroom but never coming in, even when she yearned for his comfort. Guarding her as he wandered, and also pacing out the slow beats of his own sorrow, unable to settle. The thought of Damon falling like Stefan had, his handsome face suddenly blank and still, made Elena's heart pound frantically. 'Please, Damon,' she begged.

His eyes softening, Damon sighed and brushed a finger gently over her knuckles, then pulled his hand back quickly, his jaw tightening. 'I won't do anything foolish. Remember, I'm good at taking care of myself.'

Elena started to nod gratefully, then paused as she thought through what he'd said. He hadn't promised to stay out of danger, not really. 'You can't kill anyone,' she reminded him stubbornly. 'The Guardians told you, if you kill anyone, I'll die. So there's not much point in looking for revenge.'

Damon smiled without humour, his features sharp. 'Vampires aren't human,' he said. 'I can kill Jack, and I will.'

Elena let go of his hand. Damon would never stop hunting Jack.

Damon would die on this hunt, she was sure of it. And then Elena would truly have nothing.

CHAPTER 3

Damon paced across Elena's living room, glaring at the afternoon sunlight stretching through the windows and across the floor. When he'd woken from his restless sleep an hour earlier, the apartment had already been empty.

Brushing his fingers across his chest absently, he let Elena's emotions thrum through the bond between them. Nothing had changed; he still felt the same sharp, angry grief that had brought him back to Dalcrest, that had let him know his brother was dead. But nothing new. Wherever Elena had gone, she wasn't in danger.

He ached to be out hunting Jack, to find him and tear him apart. Rage burned under his skin – how dare anyone touch his little brother. Even when he and

Stefan had hated each other, no one else had been allowed to hurt him.

But for now, Damon was keeping a low profile, guarding Elena, waiting for the right time.

Meredith had tried laying down the law to him after Stefan's funeral. 'As far as Jack knows, you're still in Europe,' she'd said. 'We need to keep it that way. You might be the best weapon we've got.'

Every line of the grey-eyed hunter's body had been tense with irritation at having to ask Damon for something; under other circumstances, this would have amused him. Meredith had no right to tell him what to do, and he had no reason to do what she asked.

But then Elena, with a desperate pleading look in her eyes, had said, 'Please, Damon. I can't lose you, too.' And Damon had agreed to do whatever she wanted.

He sighed and sat down on the couch, glancing around. He was beginning to loathe this room, pretty as it was, with its heavy antique furniture and art posters on the walls. It was decorated to Stefan's taste: dark, traditional, cosy. Stefan's taste, Stefan's possessions, Stefan's Elena.

On the table beside the couch lay a thick notebook bound in brown leather: Jack's journal, the record of the series of experiments he had done to create his new race of vampires. Damon had found it when he'd infiltrated Jack's company in Switzerland.

Near the end was a list of vampires Jack had destroyed – and a list of those he still planned to hunt down. Damon picked up the journal and turned to the long column of names. Many were vampires Damon had known over the years, their names scratched through. Near the bottom of the page, three names, not yet crossed out: *Katherine von Swartzchild. Damon Salvatore. Stefan Salvatore.*

Damon traced the names lightly with his finger, remembering how Katherine's face had paled as her life ebbed away. He felt again the sudden spike of anguished horror from Elena that had told him Stefan was dead. At least Damon had stolen the book before Jack had the opportunity to cross out their names.

Clenching his jaw, he flipped forward through its pages again. If he couldn't just go out and hunt Jack down – yet – he could still look for clues on how to defeat him.

But there was nothing new written here. He'd gone through it dozens of times. After a few minutes, he groaned softly and closed his eyes, bringing a hand up to rub his temples.

There was plenty about the weaknesses of Jack's creations, true. But the journal was a record of how Jack had overcome those flaws. Sunlight, fire, decapitation, stake to the heart: as far as Damon could tell, there was no way to kill these man-made vampires.

It was hopeless. Maybe Damon should give up, do what Elena wanted and hide.

No. His eyes snapped open and he gritted his teeth. He was *Damon Salvatore*. No mad scientist was going to defeat him.

He snapped the book closed. Any true danger to these manufactured vampires would have to be something Jack hadn't thought of.

Almost unwillingly, Damon let his gaze travel to the heavy mahogany cabinet against the wall. Stefan's talismans sat on top of it, a collection of objects from his long life. Coins, a stone cup, a watch. An apricot hair ribbon of Elena's, acquired before Stefan had even really known her, before Damon had known her at all. What would have been different, Damon wondered, if he had been the one to meet Elena first?

Damon stood and went slowly over to the cabinet, where he touched the things lightly: iron box, golden coins, ivory dagger, silken ribbon.

Damon didn't hang on to things the way Stefan had. He never saw the point of keeping objects he'd outgrown, dragging his past around the world with him.

Stefan had carried their past for him, he realised. The thought gave him a hollow feeling in his chest. With Stefan and Katherine both dead, there was no one left now who remembered Damon when he had been alive.

He drew one finger along the blade of the ivory-handled dagger and pulled his hand back with a hiss. Stefan had kept it sharp, although it had probably been centuries since he'd used it.

Their father had carried this dagger for years, Damon remembered, hanging in a sheath at his belt. A beautiful object, its fine glossy hilt curving above a well-cut, and useful, blade. He had given it to Stefan for his fifteenth birthday.

'Every gentleman should wear one,' Giuseppe Salvatore had said, grasping his younger son's shoulder affectionately. 'Not for aggression or fighting in the streets like a peasant –' Damon had felt his father's sidelong gaze light upon him, and hadn't that been as pointed as the dagger itself? '– but in case you need it. This blade is forged of the finest steel. It's served me well.'

Stefan's green eyes had shone as he looked up at their father. 'Thank you, Father,' he'd said. 'I'll treasure it.'

Lounging elegantly beside them, left out of the moment between his father and little brother, Damon had touched his own quite beautiful bone-handled dagger, and his mouth had suddenly filled with bitterness.

He blinked the memory away. He'd wasted a lot of time resenting Stefan, his sweet-faced tagalong of a baby brother.

He was wasting time now. Damon's slow heart

thumped hard, the hollow ache in his chest increasing. His earnest, loving, irritating little brother was gone. Murdered. And Damon was cowering in the shadows? His face twisted in disgust. He could imagine what their father would have said about that.

In one smooth motion, he scooped up the dagger and headed for the door. He would keep his promise to Elena; he would be careful. But he wasn't going to hide, not any more. Damon was a Salvatore – the last of the Salvatores, now – and that meant he wasn't afraid of anything.

It was time to take control of the fight. And the first thing he needed to do was to figure out where Jack might be hiding.

The river lapped gently against the small stones on its bank, sunlight glinting off its ripples. Elena instinctively moved deeper into the shade of one of the moss-covered trees by the riverside.

The rectangle of earth that marked Stefan's grave still stood out clearly. There hadn't been time yet for the soil to harden, for the grass to grow over it and erase where they'd blanketed Stefan with dirt.

It hadn't been long at all since Stefan had been alive.

A wave of anguish washed over Elena, and she dropped to her knees by the graveside. Reaching out, she placed a gentle hand on the recently turned earth.

She wanted to say something, to tell him how much

she missed him, but when she opened her mouth, all that came out was his name. 'Stefan,' she said miserably, her voice catching in her throat. 'Oh, Stefan.'

Just a couple of weeks ago, they'd been together. Not long before that, he had surprised her with the key to her old home – he'd bought the house that she'd grown up in from her Aunt Judith. 'We're going to go everywhere,' he'd told her, his hands strong and steady around hers. 'But we'll always have this to come home to.'

It turned out always lasted less than a week after that. They hadn't even had time to visit the house together. Elena dug her fingers deep into the dirt, trying not to think about Stefan's body six feet below.

'Elena?'

Bonnie came forward from the trees. Elena pulled her hands away from Stefan's grave. It seemed too intimate a gesture to let anyone see it, even Bonnie. Thank you for coming,' she said quietly, rising to her feet.

'Of course.' Bonnie's brown eyes were huge and anxious. She stepped forward and pulled Elena into a hug. 'How are you doing? We've been – Zander and I wanted to know if there was any way we could help you.'

'Actually, I think there is,' Elena told her. She took Bonnie's hand in her own and led her over to Stefan's grave.

'I keep expecting him to show up,' Bonnie admitted, her eyes fixed on the grave. 'It's hard to believe he's gone, y'know?'

No, Elena didn't know. From the moment she woke up in the morning until she finally tossed and turned her way into a restless sleep, she couldn't forget that Stefan was gone. His absence even followed her into her dreams. She didn't say that, though, just moved a little closer to Bonnie, as if she could shelter in her friend's warmth.

'Remember how you talked to me after I died?' Elena asked, squeezing Bonnie's hand in hers.

Tearing her eyes away from the ground, Bonnie looked back up at Elena. 'Oh, Elena, I don't think – '

'You managed to bring Stefan to see me,' Elena went on doggedly, holding tight to her friend's arm.

Bonnie tried to pull away. 'But you weren't supposed to be dead! Klaus had you in some kind of halfway place – you were a prisoner, not dead-dead.' She hesitated, and then asked in a low voice, 'And do you remember how the Guardians said vampires just . . . end?'

'It's worth a try, though, isn't it?' Elena said quickly. 'Guardians don't know everything, we've proved that before. If you could help me to see him, Bonnie . . .' She was holding on to Bonnie too tightly, she realised, and forced her hands to relax. 'Please,' she added quietly.

Bonnie chewed her lip. Elena could feel the moment when she gave in, her shoulders slumping. 'I don't want you to be hurt any more than you already are,' Bonnie said quietly.

'We have to try,' Elena insisted.

Bonnie hesitated, then finally nodded. 'OK.' She narrowed her eyes thoughtfully, and stepped towards the river, pulling Elena along with her. 'When I did it for Stefan, I went into a trance and made contact with you, then brought him in. But I think maybe we'll have to try something different.'

Their feet crunched over the rocky sand as Bonnie pulled Elena with her to the very edge of the river. Water lapped against their sneakers, soaking through the fabric and chilling Elena's toes.

'I want you to let me use your Power,' Bonnie said, squeezing Elena's hand. 'It'll help me search for Stefan. When I communicated with you, you came to me first, so I knew how to find you. I imagine he'll be hard to find.'

'Of course,' Elena said.

She held tightly to Bonnie's hand and tried to channel her own Power into her friend. Taking a deep, slow breath, Elena forced herself to relax until, out of the corners of her eyes, she began to see her own golden aura. It was dulled with grey patches of grief, but still stretched wide around her, entwining with the rose-pink of Bonnie's aura.

Bonnie took a deep breath of her own and fixed her eyes on the patterns of the sunlight reflecting off the water. 'Just as good as a candle for focusing,' she said absently. Elena watched as Bonnie's small face became intent, her pupils as wide as a cat's. Elena closed her own eyes.

Darkness. But ahead of her, a glimmer of rose and gold. Bonnie's aura entwined with her own, leading her on. Bonnie's small figure, very straight and determined, walked swiftly into the distance.

Elena hurried after her, her chest tight with excitement. She would see Stefan again. She could tell him how hard it was without him every day, and he would hold her in his arms and comfort her. It would be like coming home.

They walked on into the darkness, the light of their auras surrounding them both. But then, slowly, the glow of their entwined auras began to fade. Elena called out, but her voice stuck in her throat. Where was Bonnie? Elena tried to run after her, but her friend grew smaller and smaller, finally disappearing from view.

Elena stopped, half sobbing.

'Stefan!' she called. Her voice echoed back to her. 'Stefan!'

She was alone in the darkness.

Elena's eyes fluttered open. She was standing on the riverbank, her toes chilled by the lapping waves. Bonnie blinked up at her, her face pale and wet with tears.

'I'm so sorry, Elena,' she said. 'I couldn't find him. He's not anywhere we can reach.'

Elena leaned into her friend, letting Bonnie's arms circle her shoulders, and sobbed.

Bonnie felt terrible. As she toed off her damp sneakers in the entryway of her and Zander's apartment, she sniffled experimentally. Maybe spending the afternoon at the river had given her a cold. That would be an easy explanation for the rotten, hollow sensation in her chest.

But, no, if Bonnie was honest with herself, she had to admit the feeling was guilt. The first thing Elena had asked her for since Stefan had died – the only thing Elena had asked anybody for at all – and Bonnie couldn't do it.

Remembering Elena's strained smile when she thanked her for trying, Bonnie almost tripped over Zander's mud-caked work boots, catching herself with a hand against the wall. Now, the end of summer, was the time when his landscaping business planted shrubs and trees, and every day he came home absolutely filthy.

That was what Bonnie needed. Zander. He'd pull her into his arms, smelling of grass and sunshine, and tell that it was OK, that she'd done the best she could.

She heard Zander's voice and followed his low tones to the kitchen. As she turned the corner from the hallway, she stopped for a moment to simply look at him. He was standing with his back to her, all long lean muscles and tanned skin, his moonlight-blond hair curling at the nape of his neck, still damp with sweat. They'd been together for years now, but the sight of him still sometimes made her want to melt into a puddle on the floor.

'I *know*,' he said sharply into the phone. 'I'm not changing my mind.'

'Hey,' she whispered, stepping forward and lightly brushing her fingers across his back. Zander jumped.

'Bonnie's here,' he said tightly, turning around to face her. 'I have to go. I'll call you later.' He clicked the phone off.

'Who was that?' Bonnie asked, leaning forward for a kiss. Zander's lips met hers, warm and soft. When he pulled away, though, he avoided her eyes.

'No one important,' he said. 'You want pizza for dinner? Jared told me the secret of that crust he makes. Cornmeal.'

'Sounds good,' Bonnie said, but she couldn't help frowning. 'Are you OK?'

Zander looked at her then, and his face split into a smile, his sky-blue eyes crinkling at the corners. 'Never better,' he said.

'OK.' Bonnie smiled back tentatively. Zander's gaze had skidded away from hers again, and his shoulders were stiff.

She pushed away the tickle of worry at the back of her mind. They'd all been tense since Stefan's death. There was nothing more to it than that.

Thinking of Stefan, Bonnie sighed, and Zander turned back towards her, instantly alert. 'What's up?' he asked, his face full of concern.

'I tried to contact Stefan today so Elena could say goodbye. But I couldn't find him.'

'Oh, Bonnie,' he said. And just as she'd known he would, he put an arm around her shoulders. Bonnie automatically snuggled into it, taking comfort in his strength. 'She knows you did everything you could,' Zander went on reassuringly. 'There's nothing you wouldn't do for her.'

But Elena had looked so broken, Bonnie thought. Nothing like the proud girl Bonnie had known since they were kids. Elena loved Stefan with everything she had, and now she was left with nothing.

Bonnie shivered and cuddled against Zander. 'I love you,' she told him. Without a word, Zander pulled her even closer.

CHAPTER

4

The sun was just beginning to sink behind Dalcrest's science lab, sending long golden rays across the college's lawns. On the branch of a maple tree overhanging the path, a large crow stretched out its glossy blue-black wings. Its gaze was fixed intently on the side entrance to the lab.

Damon shifted his talons along the branch, then smoothed an errant feather with his beak. He'd been searching Dalcrest all day, in both crow and human form.

Assuming that Jack was using medical facilities to get the supplies he needed to create his monstrosities, there were a limited number of possible locations in town. There had been no sign of Jack at the busy hospital or the quieter medical practices, most closed for the weekend. So now Damon was at campus, staking out the Dalcrest science lab. It was a long shot, he figured, that Jack would still be this close to where he was last seen, but he had to try. Stefan was dead, and all Damon could think of right now was finding the monster who'd killed him.

The campus was deserted; it was the time of year when the summer students had finally gone home and the professors hadn't yet begun to prepare for their fall classes. But now a stocky, dark-haired man was coming out of the science lab, and Damon straightened on his branch. The man, who was wearing a pack on his back and carrying a large box, fit the description he'd gotten of Jack – right colouring, build, age – although probably a hundred other humans in Dalcrest would fit the same description. Clicking his beak thoughtfully, Damon sent out a tendril of Power to see if he could find anything that suggested the man was other than human.

Was there the tiniest shift in his aura? These vampires had learned to shield themselves, to appear human so as not to alert their prey. But here he would think he was alone, no one watching him but a bird in a tree. Now that Damon was concentrating his attention fully on this man, there seemed to be something not quite natural, something wrong shimmering through his protective mask. Damon spread his wings wide. *Got you now*, he thought, rather smugly, as he fluttered quietly down on to the path behind the man, shifting to his own form as he landed.

Damon's perfectly polished black boots hit the path without a sound, but Jack whipped around immediately. Definitely a vampire.

'Hello,' Damon said, giving a blindingly bright smile. Jack's face twitched in confusion, and Damon attacked, knocking him to the ground and sending the box flying out of Jack's hands. 'We haven't met,' he growled, pinning Jack's shoulders hard against the path. 'But I hear you've been looking for me.'

Fangs extending, Damon tore at the other vampire's throat. There had to be some way to kill him. If there was one thing Damon knew for certain, it was that every being, natural or supernatural, had a weakness. You just had to know how to find it.

Maybe if he could get Jack's head off fast enough that the other vampire couldn't heal . . . Blood filled his mouth, acidic and chemical, and Damon spat it to the side, grimacing. With a grunt of effort, Jack managed to flip Damon off, and they were both on their feet in an instant, circling each other. Jack fumbled at his side and pulled a stake from his pocket.

Damon wasn't worried. He had a weapon of his own. Eyeing Jack, he drew Stefan's ivory-handled dagger – his dagger, now – and held it guardedly, his arms spread. The dagger was poised to strike in his right hand, his left hand open and ready to grapple with his opponent. Usually he preferred to rely on his own hands and teeth in a fight, but using Stefan's dagger seemed fitting. The lessons of dagger fighting he'd learned centuries earlier all came back to him now.

Watching Jack carefully, Damon waited for an opening. He was pretty sure he could take the false vampire. The vampires who had hunted Damon, who had killed Katherine, had been strong and fast, but no faster or stronger than Damon and Katherine. The problem had been that there were too many of them, and that they didn't stay dead. Jack by himself should be easy.

Damon feinted to the left. Jack flinched, and Damon moved in on the right, slashing a deep cut along Jack's stomach. Jack growled, a low, animal sound, and thrust his stake towards Damon's heart. He missed, and it sank into Damon's shoulder instead, tearing a gaping wound in his flesh.

Sucking in a shocked breath, Damon stumbled for a second before he caught himself. Jack quickly stabbed him again with the stake, this time in the side. Twisting, Damon slashed down, cutting a long bloody stripe along Jack's leg. They grappled hand-to-hand for a moment, both breathing hard, then shoved apart, coming to a halt a few feet from each other.

'Damon Salvatore,' Jack said, smiling as if they were friends. 'You're the clever brother, aren't you? Not like Stefan.'

Damon suppressed the hot flare of rage that rose up at his brother's name. It wouldn't do him any good to get angry now. He had to keep cool if he was going to defeat Jack. He was stronger than Damon had thought he would be, stronger than the other man-made vampires Damon had fought. A trickle of blood ran down Damon's side, and he realised his shirt was soaked with it. Blood was pulsing from the wounds the stake had left in him even as his flesh began to try to knit itself together.

Jack's clothes were ruined, too, but Damon saw that beneath the slashed fabric his skin was already whole again. He healed as fast as his minions had.

Damon leapt at Jack, moving before the other vampire could prepare, and sank his fangs into one side of Jack's throat. Not delicately, as he did while feeding, but with a rough, tearing bite. He worked his teeth against one side of Jack's throat as he brought his dagger up to stab repeatedly at the other, ripping the dagger from side to side. If he could do enough damage . . .

But there was more resistance than there should be to his bite and the dagger's thrust. Jack's skin was thicker and stronger than a human's – or even an ordinary vampire's. Damon shook with a sudden shock as Jack sank the stake into him again, through the back this time. The tip grated painfully on one of Damon's ribs. He ripped more fiercely at Jack's throat, but Jack's next blow knocked the wind out of him.

Letting go of Jack, Damon staggered backward. He wiped at his mouth with the back of one hand and realised blood – his own blood – was running down his chin. He coughed and choked again.

Jack must have nicked Damon's lung. He needed time to heal before he could fight again; he needed to feed.

'Huh. Maybe not the clever brother after all,' Jack said. The wounds on his neck had already closed, Damon saw with dismay.

Damon backed up a few steps, keeping his eyes on Jack, who moved closer. A bubble of blood rose in Damon's throat and he spat, staining the path with a blossom of bright red. There was a wall behind him, he realised. Jack was blocking him in.

Jack swung the pack off his back and reached inside, pulling something out. Something metal, with a grip and a nozzle—

A flamethrower? Damon drew on his last reserves of strength and leapt to one side, the flames so close he felt them scorch his jeans.

'Thoughtful of you to come right to me,' Jack said, aiming the flamethrower again. 'I assumed you were still in Paris.'

Damon gathered his last vestiges of energy to dodge again. *Like a rat in a trap*, he thought dimly. He tried to tense for another leap, but his body gave out and he staggered to the side, his legs collapsing underneath him. Black spots danced before his eyes. His mouth was full of blood.

Jack gripped the nozzle of the flamethrower in both hands and lifted it up, taking aim – and then, suddenly, flew backward. Like a rag doll shot by a slingshot, he sailed through the air, hitting the side of the building behind him with a satisfying crunch. He slid into the grass, a limp, broken form.

Damon blinked in dazed shock. After a moment, he thought to look behind him.

Over the top of the hill behind the science building, Elena appeared, her face coldly ferocious, her Guardian Powers clearly in full force. 'My hero,' Damon muttered wryly, and his knees buckled.

Damon blinked back to full consciousness and found himself lying propped up against the trunk of a tree, Elena's arms around him. She smelled sweet and her skin was soft; Damon let himself luxuriate in lying next to her for a moment before he licked the blood away from his lips and coughed.

'Are you all right?' Elena asked as he tried to sit up.

'Not particularly,' Damon said weakly, and patted along his chest. The wounds were only half closed, and he was still bleeding. He couldn't breathe properly. 'Where's Jack?'

'He got away while I was helping you,' Elena admitted.

'Next time, then.' Damon coughed again, wincing.

'What were you thinking, Damon?' In contrast to her stern words, her hands stroking his hair were gentle and her face was creased with concern. 'You promised to be careful, and then you go chasing after Jack.'

Damon squinted up at her. 'I had my reasons,' he said. He couldn't talk about how hard it was to do nothing when Stefan was dead. Anyway, Elena knew. She could feel it through their connection; he didn't have the strength to hide his thoughts from her right now.

'We'll talk later,' Elena said. 'First, we need to get you back on your feet.' Damon coughed again, and her eyes widened at the spatter of blood that came from his mouth. 'You need to feed,' she said instantly, pulling her hair aside. 'Here.'

She smelled so good, the blood pulsing beneath her skin less than an inch from his lips. Damon recalled clearly how sweet and rich Elena's blood had always been – the best he'd ever tasted, something special. He could imagine gulping it down, feeling it heal his wounds and fill him with warmth and Power.

Still, he hesitated. She was his brother's, bound to Stefan now by death even more securely than in life. It would be different to drink her blood now, feeling her grief over Stefan. 'Are you sure?' he murmured.

Elena nodded, her face white and strained, but determined. 'I'm sure,' she said, and pulled him closer.

Damon couldn't resist any longer. *I'm sorry, little brother*. He slipped his canines beneath Elena's skin as gently as he could and teased them lightly back and forth, encouraging the flow of her blood into his mouth. Those first swallows were warm and sweet, as heady as wine, filling him with life. He could feel the blood streaming down his throat as he gulped, quenching his thirst and hunger, helping to heal his injuries. The stab wound in his back closed and the pain disappeared. Elena was sharing her Power with him, and he would be strong again soon.

His mind brushed hers, and he had such a strong feeling of Elena, stronger even than came through their bond. He wanted to dive into her, curl up in her essence. There was grief there, and passion – and, abruptly, an overwhelming sense from Elena of off limits. Damon pulled back as if he'd been burned. He tried to shut his own mind off, to give her some privacy. It was like pressing your body against another person's, but both averting your eyes.

Still, images and emotions came through their bond. Frustration. Worry. Fear. And a deep, painful sense of loss. A picture of Stefan's ivory-handled dagger, clutched in Damon's bloodstained hand, came to him from Elena, and he winced. The dagger belonged to her as much as it did to Damon.

I had to take it, he told her silently.

I know, came back to him immediately, and with it a

wave of sorrow and of love. She was torn apart inside, but she was there. He still had her. Damon drank deeply, letting Elena's blood, Elena's sorrow, Elena's love, fill him once again.

CHAPTER
5

'But is Damon OK?' Alaric asked, his fork suspended halfway to his mouth.

'Damon's always all right,' Meredith said swiftly. That wasn't quite true, of course – Damon had died once – but there was so much going on at the steakhouse Alaric had brought her to that she couldn't concentrate on their conversation. Alaric had thought it would be nice for them to have a real date night, but Meredith wasn't sure she was going to be able to cope with the crowd.

The waitress set down their sides – potato, creamed spinach, salad – and Meredith flinched. It was one of her favourite meals, but it smelled terrible, cloying, like sweet-rotting vegetation. The waitress herself, though, smelled delicious, warm and salty and ripe. Meredith averted her eyes and took a tiny sip of ice water. She was always thirsty these days, but if she drank too much water, it made her sick. It wasn't what her body wanted.

She took a deep breath and concentrated. *I am stronger than this*, she told herself. She hadn't fed, not even from an animal. If she drank blood, the vampire inside her would get the upper hand, defeat the real Meredith. Tears prickled at the corners of her eyes, and she took another sip of water. The vampire would never be the real her. There had to be a way to fix this.

Behind her, plates clattered and Meredith jumped. She could hear twenty different conversations, all overlapping one another – *why don't you think it's a good idea, I'd better call the sitter and let her know, the client isn't always right, you know what I mean, I don't think she's as hot as she thinks she is, we'd been trying and trying, did you see the preview for, not potatoes, rice, well, why did you come, then* – on and on, and it was making it really hard to concentrate. There was a sudden, raucous burst of laughter from the table in the corner, and Meredith flinched again. If this was how vampires experienced the world, she didn't know how they ever managed to focus.

And the smells. Half of them were sickening – the food, someone's overly floral perfume, the harsh cleanser they'd used on the carpet – but the warm, living smell of the other diners was tantalising.

It was way too bright in here. Meredith pressed a hand to her temple.

'Are you OK?' Alaric asked, his golden-brown eyes warm with concern. 'I thought this would take our minds off everything that's been going on.'

Determinedly, Meredith yanked her attention away from a disturbing medical conversation three tables away. 'I'm great,' she answered, forcing a smile. 'You're right, this is a nice night away from it all.'

She couldn't tell him. Every time she tried to open her mouth and confide in Alaric, the one person she loved most in the world, it felt like a rough hand was squeezing her lungs, leaving her breathless and silent. He'd stood by her through so much. She was a hunter, with all the danger that entailed. She'd had to kill her own brother and it had scarred her, made her angry and silent for a while. Law school ate up so much of her time and energy. She was uptight and hard to please. They had survived all that, but this – this was different. She was going to fix this, somehow. He would never have to know.

Alaric smiled. 'Try your steak,' he suggested. 'Rare enough for you?'

Hesitantly, she picked up her fork and knife and cut into it. She did like her steaks rare, she always had. It was red and juicy inside, almost bloody. She was so hungry. And Alaric was watching her, his forehead furrowing into a frown of concern. Meredith cut off a piece of meat and put it into her mouth.

Bile rose in her throat, and Meredith stifled a gag. It was foul, like she'd bitten into something rotten. Pretending to wipe her lips, Meredith spat the bite into her napkin and smiled half-heartedly at Alaric. Her mouth felt coated in rot, and she tried to discreetly scrape her tongue against her teeth.

She'd seen Damon eat human food at least a hundred times. Not very much, but he'd seemed to enjoy it. Even if she was different now, why couldn't she eat?

Meredith straightened her shoulders, reminding herself that she was strong. She could fight this. If science could cause her to feel this way, then science must be able to fix her.

She had gone back to where Jack had operated on her, but he'd been gone, the operating room just another bland office in a medical centre. She hadn't dared to try the phone number and address on the business card he had given her.

Alaric was saying something, gesturing happily with one hand as he talked, eating more of his own steak. Meredith blinked at him and tried to smile and nod. She couldn't hear him properly, his voice drowned out by the millions of noises all around them and the welter of scents filling her nose.

Alaric's smell in particular, warm and fresh. She could hear his heart again, pounding steadily in her ears, her own heart speeding to match it. Her canines slowly began to lengthen, and Meredith clamped her mouth shut. She couldn't stop staring at the side of his throat, at the tendon and vein there. She imagined leaping across the table and sinking her fangs into him. She could almost feel how satisfying it would be for Alaric's flesh to rip beneath her teeth.

Meredith swallowed hard and closed her eyes. *I have to fix this*, she thought desperately.

The ball slid neatly into the pins, knocking them all down in a perfect strike. 'Wooo!' Jasmine whooped. 'I am the champion!' Her long dark curls flew out around her as she spun, arms raised in a victory pose.

'Yes, you're completely awesome,' Matt said, rolling his eyes. 'I'm still winning, though.'

'How can that be possible?' Jasmine said with mock surprise, looking up at the scoreboard over the lane. 'Are you cheating?'

Matt laughed. 'How could I be cheating?' he asked. 'I roll the ball, the ball knocks down the pins, the computer counts how many I knocked down. I've gotten five strikes and you've gotten one. Don't be a sore loser.'

Jasmine raised an eyebrow at him. 'Everyone you know is magic. Bonnie or Elena would spell a scoreboard for you any time.'

'I repeat. Sore. Loser,' Matt said, smiling at her, admiring the flush of her cheeks and her wide, bright eyes. Her curls flew loose and wild around her shoulders, and Matt just wanted to bury his face in them, breathe in the mint-and-citrus scent of her shampoo.

Instead, he stepped closer and brushed his hand against hers. It occurred to him suddenly that, despite every terrible thing that had happened lately, he was happy. He couldn't help feeling guilty. Stefan had been his friend, his comrade-in-arms, and now he was dead.

What kept him from feeling guiltier, though, was that Stefan would have wanted him to be happy. Stefan had approved of Jasmine. 'A very nice girl,' Stefan had called her once, raising a glass and giving Matt that faint, privately amused smile he saved for his more human moments.

And wasn't it Matt's turn to find love, finally? He'd spent so long hopelessly infatuated with Elena, and then he'd fallen for poor, doomed Chloe.

After the bleakness of Chloe's death, Jasmine had been like a gift: funny, smart and beautiful. And she loved Matt back.

A month ago, he'd had to let her know about the true darkness beneath the logical, serene place that had always been her reality. His worst fear had come true: Jasmine had run away from him.

But she had come back. Because she loved him, and because she wanted to help fight that darkness. Now she was able to joke about the supernatural craziness that suffused his life, and he felt closer to her than ever.

The crash of bowling pins in the next lane brought Matt out of his thoughts and he smiled at Jasmine, brushing a long curl away from her face.

'I love you,' he told her, his eyes steady on hers.

Jasmine's face brightened with pleasure, and she reached up to catch his hand, her warm fingers entwining with his. 'I love you, too,' she said. 'I'm all in now. No more secrets.' She looked determined, her mouth firmly set. She meant it.

Jasmine's ball rattled in the ball return, and Matt slid an arm around her waist as she reached for it. 'I'll share one secret now,' he said, dropping a kiss on the back of her neck. 'The secret of my athletic skill. Let me show you my moves, lady.' He slid his hand down to hers to help support the ball and moved in closer.

'Oldest line in the book,' Jasmine said, leaning back against him, smirking, her serious tone abandoned. Her hair was soft against his cheek. 'Go ahead, show me everything.'

CHAPTER
6

'Meredith, call me,' Elena said. She clicked off the phone, dropping it on to the passenger seat beside her. It had been a couple of days since she'd been able to reach Meredith. Of course her friend was busy – between law school and patrolling for vampires, she was always busy – but she usually kept in close contact with Elena. They worked together, Elena thought, and it was bewildering to have Meredith drop out of touch.

Elena's palm itched suddenly, and she rubbed it against the steering wheel as she drove.

Without warning, a cool chill, like a trickle of cold water, ran down her back. Elena jerked, automatically pressing down on the gas pedal. There was someone following her, she was certain. Her eyes flicked up to the rear-view mirror.

A dark SUV crept up closely behind her. She couldn't make out the driver's face.

Elena let her eyes shift, using her Guardian Power to search for nearby auras, and blinked in surprise. The aura of whoever was driving was pure white, spreading out around the SUV in a great cloud of light. Beautiful, really, but not human. Not vampire or werewolf either.

And it was aggravatingly familiar. No wonder the figure-eight-shaped scar on her hand had itched – the cut Mylea had given her was probably some sort of homing device. It would be like the Guardians to mark Elena in a way that made her easy to track.

Elena pulled over on to the shoulder and turned off the engine. Climbing out of the car, she felt her heart beat faster at the sight of the tall woman with smooth blonde hair.

Mylea herself stepped out of the SUV, the Celestial Guardian who had initiated Elena into her own Guardianship, and who had bound her and Damon together.

Celestial Guardians were not her favourite people, not by a long shot. Self-righteous, judgemental and dangerous were about the right words for them. But they were also Powerful. If Mylea had come here about Jack and his vampires, she could give Elena Power that would help her defeat them. Elena would be able to take revenge for Stefan. She could protect Damon.

Elena took a deep breath and walked towards the

Guardian, roadside gravel crunching beneath her feet.

'Elena Gilbert,' the tall, golden-haired Guardian said levelly as soon as they were face-to-face. Her eyes, the same dark blue as Elena's own, were cool and assessing. 'The Celestial Court requires your service. It is time for your next Task.'

'We've been looking for Jack Daltry,' Elena told her. 'He killed Stefan, and countless others, and we don't know where he's hiding. Can you help us?'

Mylea's forehead creased slightly, a small line appearing between her perfectly arched brows. 'That is not why I've come. Jack Daltry is not your concern,' she said.

'Not my concern?' Outrage flooded over Elena, and she clenched her fists involuntarily. Biting back her anger, she tried to speak as calmly as Mylea did. 'He killed Stefan. That makes him my concern.'

Mylea's frown deepened. 'It is not your place to avenge the death of vampires,' she said. 'Your duty is to protect the human race from the supernatural, not the other way around.'

'I know!' Elena's voice was almost a shout, and she took a deep breath and forced her fists to unclench. Emotion would do nothing to influence Mylea. 'But Jack is a danger to humans,' she argued, more calmly. 'He's been changing them into vampires. And he feeds on humans, just like any other vampire.'

Celestial Guardians didn't shrug, in Elena's

experience – it was too human a gesture – but the tilt of Mylea's head as she listened gave the same impression: What Elena was saying might be true, but it was irrelevant. 'Everything in the universe balances eventually, but Jack Daltry and his creations are not your responsibility,' she said. 'They are not supernatural.'

'They're vampires,' Elena said, losing her grip on her temper again.

'They are an imitation of true vampires, created by a human,' Mylea said sternly.

Elena gritted her teeth and glared at the Celestial Guardian. 'I had forgotten how fixated Guardians are on technicalities.'

Mylea ignored this. 'You have other duties,' she said.

She took Elena's hand – her own hand was cold, as cold as any vampire's, Elena realised – and turned it palm upwards. Elena's scar was itching more than ever, and shimmering silver against the pale skin of her palm. Mylea ran a finger across it, and Elena shuddered. Her anger was ebbing under Mylea's touch, she realised, and wondered if Mylea was using her own Power to calm Elena. She yanked her hand out of the Guardian's grip.

'You swore a blood oath,' Mylea said, her gold-flecked blue eyes fixed on Elena's, 'to obey the Celestial Court's instructions.'

'I know.' Elena sighed, resigned. There was no use in fighting Mylea. This was what she was made for, to protect people. It didn't mean she couldn't concentrate on finding Jack as well. 'Tell me what you want.'

'An old vampire has come to this part of the world. She's been feeding on humans and killing them,' Mylea said. 'We've known of her for a long time, but she's only gotten more dangerous the older she gets. She kills for pleasure now, not just for food, and she needs to be stopped. Her name is Siobhan.' She abruptly fell silent, and Elena's palm immediately stopped itching.

Elena waited a moment, but Mylea seemed to be finished. 'That's it? You can't tell me anything else?'

Mylea tilted her head again. 'What would you like to know?'

'Anything. Where she is? What she looks like?'

Turning to walk back towards her car, Mylea spoke back over her shoulder. 'You'll have the Power to find her and to defeat her when you need to. Have faith in yourself.' When she reached her SUV, she glanced at Elena again. 'One thing I will tell you. Siobhan is very clever, and, unlike most of the Old Ones you have hunted, the long years of her life have not driven the more passionate human emotions out of her.'

Elena straightened her shoulders and lifted her chin defiantly. 'I'm still going to hunt Jack.'

'It's not necessary, but we know you will pursue your own way,' Mylea said calmly. 'Your attention should, however, be elsewhere. Use caution, Elena. Remember who you are.'

Mylea swung the door of her SUV open. As she stepped into the car, there was a bright flash of white light and Elena closed her eyes against it automatically. When she opened them again a second later, the SUV, and Mylea with it, were gone. The side of the highway was empty. A breeze, chilly with the first signs of autumn, lifted Elena's hair, and she shivered, rubbing absently at her scar.

CHAPTER 7

Damon slipped from shadow to shadow, from alleyway to darkened doorway. The main street of Dalcrest was almost deserted this time of night – occasionally a car's headlights swept quickly across the fronts of the closed shops and restaurants, and one or two late wanderers hurried down the sidewalks. But he made sure the few people he encountered did not see him.

Stealth was one of his best talents, Damon thought with a small private smile as he lingered in the shadows of a storefront awning, his back pressed against the building's cold brick. Thanks to Elena's blood, he'd recovered from the beating he'd taken at Jack's hands the day before, and he felt strong and fierce.

He ran his tongue across his lips, remembering. Elena's blood had tasted so sweet. She'd shielded herself against him, but no matter – she was filled with tenderness for Damon, he had felt it through their bond, mixed with her grief and love for Stefan.

Stefan. Damon winced, gritting his teeth. Jack had to pay. He was going to be clever about it this time, though, he told himself sternly. No leaping into action without getting a full picture of the situation. He would have to be patient. Not, unfortunately, one of his best talents.

Damon narrowed his eyes thoughtfully. He was following just a trace of wrongness, something he'd sensed that felt slightly off – similar to what he'd sensed from Jack. His nose wrinkled. There was something acidic about the almost-human scent. Like a drop of something sour in a glass of water.

It was one of Jack's synthetic vampires, he was almost sure, hunting a human. The creature was about two blocks away. He let it cross another street before he pushed off the building to follow, melting into the night. If he could catch the vampire, he could learn more about what Jack was up to and where he was hiding. Maybe he could even figure out how to kill them.

Hurrying down the street, Damon kept his senses pinned on the figures ahead. The synthetic vampire was too loud and yet hesitant. It was a girl, he realised, listening to the weight of her feet pattering along behind the human, sometimes fast and close as if she was getting ready to pounce, sometimes slowing as if she was almost ready to let her victim go. *Inexperienced*, Damon thought. *Frightened*. Jack must have made this one recently.

He stretched out his Power, listening, trying to sense the minds of the vampire and victim. There it was again, that flash of something almost human, but just slightly off. This one wasn't as good at hiding it yet as Jack was, more evidence that the vampire was freshly made.

The footsteps suddenly stopped, and Damon heard a cut-off shriek. There was a surge of fear – the human – and he quickened his pace. A feeding vampire would be distracted and easier to catch.

The fear in the air drew him towards a deserted parking lot behind a Mexican restaurant. The restaurant was closed for the night, but Damon could still smell the tacos and enchiladas as he rounded the corner of the building. And, overpoweringly, the scent of blood. Damon licked his lips, his canines automatically lengthening. His mouth was watering, and he *wanted*.

But he couldn't drink. He couldn't take an unwilling human, not without hurting Elena. He would never hurt her.

The synthetic vampire and her victim were almost concealed by a wide-spreading tree at the edge of the parking lot. The victim, a young woman, was struggling feebly, whimpering.

Silently, Damon slipped closer to the entangled figures. Balancing on the balls of his feet, he was ready to leap, to take the young false vampire down. Closer . . . closer still . . .

He crouched to spring, and then froze. Something familiar about the scent. And the way the vampire moved, smooth as a predator, her long dark hair pulled back at the nape of her neck. Shock ran through him like lightning as his mind caught up with his senses, and he was frozen for a moment.

Then he dashed forward and pulled the vampire off her victim with one hand. 'Meredith?'

Meredith Sulez – vampire hunter, always composed, always contemptuous of Damon, even when they fought side-by-side – swung around to face him. He couldn't stop staring, trying to make some sense of what he was seeing. Meredith's thick black eyelashes were wet with tears and bright blood was smeared across her mouth and down her chin.

She gave a quick, broken sob, her eyes dropping as her face coloured with shame. 'Damon,' she said, pleading. 'Damon, I didn't mean to. I've kept myself from feeding for so long, and I just couldn't stop this time. I don't want to kill her. I can't – I can't let her go like this—'

He swallowed and pushed away his shock. Meredith was clinging tightly to her victim, who seemed close to unconscious, her head sagging on Meredith's shoulder. Of course she couldn't influence the girl to make her forget: Jack's vampires had no magic or

Power, they were creatures of science.

'*Please*,' Meredith begged, bringing her desperate gaze up to meet Damon's. She was biting her lip nervously, and a thin trail of her own blood trickled down her chin.

Slipping a cool mask over his surprise – *When did this happen? How could I not have known?* – Damon heaved a theatrical sigh and tugged the human out of Meredith's arms. 'Wake up,' he said, and shook her gently. The girl's head bobbled from side to side, her short hair sweeping forward across her cheeks. Meredith had really made a mess of her victim's neck – it was raw and ripped, blood still streaming out. Damon wrinkled his nose fastidiously. 'Come on, now.' He shook her again, until she blinked blearily up at him.

Efficiently, Damon bit his own wrist and pressed it against the girl's lips. He forced her to drink a few swallows, enough to make the bites on her throat begin to heal. 'That's enough.' Without waiting for an answer, he stroked his Power along her mind, pushing for obedience. 'You won't remember what happened. You were out late, and you fell, that's how you hurt your neck. Everything's fine. Go home.'

The girl stared at him blankly and dragged her tongue across her dry lips. 'I have to go home,' she muttered. 'I was out too late.'

'Good girl,' Damon said, setting her on her feet and straightening her top. It was a pity about the bloodstains, but there was nothing he could do. 'Go on.'

The girl nodded and staggered off through the parking lot. Damon watched her go and then turned his attention to Meredith.

She was staring at him, her eyes wide and horrified, her chest heaving with panicky panting breaths. Damon could feel warmth radiating off her, and her heart was pounding hard. If Damon hadn't known better – if he hadn't seen her long, sharp canines and sensed that little bit of wrongness under her false aura, he would have thought Meredith was still human.

'So . . .' he said, enjoying her distress just a little bit, now that his shock had faded. 'What's new with you?'

Meredith gulped unhappily. 'I was just so hungry,' she said, her voice strained.

Damon shrugged, keeping his expression bland. 'You don't need to explain to me, hunter,' he said. 'How long since Jack changed you?'

Meredith rubbed at her face, trying to wipe away the blood and only smearing it across her cheek. 'A week,' she said, her eyes downcast. It felt odd, seeing Meredith so humbled. 'He was working on me before that, taking me in the middle of the night. I thought I was dreaming. I couldn't see his face.'

Damon nodded. 'Does anyone else know?' he asked. It wouldn't be the first time that they'd kept him out of the loop, but he couldn't believe Elena had known. He would have sensed her shock through the bond between them, and he'd felt nothing but her constant, aching grief.

Eyes widening in horror, Meredith grabbed the front of his shirt, pulling him close to her. 'You can't tell them,' she said fiercely. 'No one else can know. I'm going to find some way to reverse it.'

Damon unwrapped Meredith's fingers from his shirt. With a little thrill, he realised that Meredith's predicament could be good. He could use this. 'Fine,' he told her. 'I won't breathe a word. But there's something I want you to do.'

Meredith's eyes narrowed. It was admirable, Damon thought, how she could go from a quivering wreck to sharply suspicious, pulling herself together in an instant. 'What do you want, Damon?'

'Don't worry,' he assured her with a bitter laugh. 'It won't hurt. Probably.' She flinched, and he sighed, feeling guilty. 'I want you to connect with Jack,' he went on, in a softer tone. 'He made you for a reason. Surely he must want you to work with him.'

Meredith's mouth opened in an automatic denial, and then she stopped. 'You want me to spy on him for you,' she said thoughtfully.

'If we're going to hunt him, hunter, we need eyes on the inside,' Damon told her. 'So, yes, I want you to spy. Where he's hiding, how many of . . . you there are, what he's planning. How to kill him. You said once that I might be the best weapon we had, but I think you are.'

Meredith's face was still streaked with blood and tears, but she wasn't crying any more. Her eyes, no longer full of shame, were speculative as she thought through the nuances of Damon's idea. She'd always been practical, this hunter, Damon thought, and was surprised by a flare of affection. Meredith wasn't his friend, but he did respect her, which was more than he could say for most humans – or vampires.

The corners of the hunter's mouth went up in a smile – a small one, but a real one. 'A secret weapon? That I can do.'

A weapon, Damon thought. He finally had a weapon against Jack. *No, not a weapon*, he corrected himself, as Meredith looked up at him and smiled in grim determination. *An ally.*

CHAPTER

8

Elena knew she was dreaming. She'd had this dream before.

The apartment stretched out before her, shadowed and deserted. 'Stefan?' she called uneasily. Her voice sounded small in her own ears.

As she walked down the endless hall in search of Stefan, the lights snapped off behind her, one after the other, leaving pools of darkness. At the end of the hall, the bedroom door was closed. A tendril of worry curled inside her. There was something wrong, something about Stefan, but she couldn't quite remember what it was.

'Stefan?' She already knew what would be behind the door – a dark, empty room, the bedroom curtains billowing in the breeze from the open windows. No

Stefan. No one anywhere, just loneliness and silence. Full of dread, she slowly lifted one hand to twist the knob.

This time, though, everything changed.

Instead of her familiar bedroom, the door opened to reveal a room she had never seen before.

Inside, a fire burned in a large stone fireplace, throwing flickering shadows across the log walls. It was warm and cosy, but the woman sitting on the couch looked as cold as ice.

She was wearing a long white dress, and her dark hair hung past her shoulders. Her blue eyes were looking straight at Elena. Elena's heart pounded in terror, and yet, there was something that wouldn't let her leave. But the woman didn't move. Blue eyes gazed straight through Elena and off into the distance.

Of course, Elena realised, she wasn't really there. This was a dream, and the woman couldn't see her.

No longer afraid to stare, she looked the woman over. She was young, maybe in her twenties, and beautiful in an unusual way. Skin so pale Elena could see the blue veins running underneath, and oddly tilted, large, light-blue eyes. The woman's hair spilled in an inky cloud over her shoulders. Her eyebrows arched dramatically dark against that pale skin. Her lips were red.

Snow White, Elena thought, remembering the fairy tale she had read to her little sister Margaret not too long ago. *The Queen said, I wish I had a child with skin as white as this cold snow, and hair as black as this ebony needle, and lips as red as my hot blood.*

As soon as she thought the word 'blood', there was an uncomfortable itch at the back of Elena's mind.

Elena focused her Power, intent on seeing the woman's aura. As her Guardian vision slotted into place, she had to grab at the doorframe, holding on so hard that the edges of the door cut into her hand.

The woman's aura was the bright red of fresh blood, and it spread far, half filling the room. Elena had never seen an aura so large and vivid, and it reeked of Power and violence. Vampire. A real one, not one of Jack's creations.

Just then, those pale, tilted eyes shifted, and met Elena's. And the woman's blood-red lips curled into a smile.

Elena sat up with a jolt, gasping in surprise. She was lying in her own big – too big, too empty – bed. Her mattress was soft, her pillows plumped up under her head. Words were completely clear in her mind, as if she had just spoken them. *Get up now*. Without stopping to think, she climbed out of bed and padded across the floor to the window.

The moon was full and sailing high over the apartment buildings on the other side of the street. Beyond them, Elena could see the blood-red path of an aura hanging in the air, leading further into town.

Siobhan. It must be. Already, she could feel the insistent pull of her Guardian Powers. She had to find Siobhan and kill her, before anyone else died. No time to waste. If she lost the trail of Siobhan's aura, it might take weeks before she found it again. Weeks when the vampire could be murdering innocent people. Hurrying, Elena slipped her feet into sandals and ran out the door of her apartment.

She had pounded down the stairs and out the front door of her building before she realised she was still dressed in her long, lacy, white nightgown. It didn't matter, she decided. She would just scope out Siobhan's situation, find the room from her dream – a cabin, it looked like – and drive away. She would come back later, with Damon.

At the thought of Damon, something inside Elena twisted. When he had held her in his arms and slipped his fangs into her throat, it had felt so right, like a homecoming. She couldn't betray Stefan, not now. But she had always cared for Damon. Stefan had known that.

Driving her little Mini Cooper through the mostly empty roads of Dalcrest, Elena kept glancing up, following the smoky red tendrils of Siobhan's aura. She expected them to lead straight through town and off into the hills nearby, places you might find a cosy cabin like the one Elena had dreamed of. But instead the trail led to the drive-in movie theatre at the edge of town.

Elena had never been there, but she had heard about it – it had just opened earlier that summer, playing old movies to lure in families and the student crowd. The marquee outside read:

DOUBLE MIDNIGHT FEATURE

DRACULA

SON OF DRACULA

Ironic, Elena thought. It seemed like Siobhan had a sense of humour.

An old black-and-white film flickered on a huge screen, just visible over the top of the fence. Elena pulled up to the gate, and a white-haired man came out of his little booth to take her money. 'First movie's almost over,' he said genially. 'Half price, sweetheart.'

Elena thanked him and pulled the car into the lot below the big screen. There were only about twenty cars there. As she parked, she saw Siobhan's aura trace across the lot to a big old boat of a black car parked near the back.

Siobhan was leaning against the car.

In a moment, everything in Elena went on alert. She slammed open the door of her car, fumbling off her seatbelt, her gaze fixed on Siobhan. The vampire was tall and elegant lounging there, her long black hair cascading down her shoulders just as in Elena's dream. As Elena watched, she wiped her mouth daintily with the back of one pale hand and raised her other hand in greeting, fanning her fingers at Elena in a ta-ta gesture.

Elena's feet hit the asphalt and the doors of her Power flew open. She felt something burst from her, a huge silent wave of Power crashing towards Siobhan, ready to drag the vampire under.

But it was too late. By the time Elena reached the car, the vampire was gone, moving so fast that Elena saw only a blur. Power from Elena hit the side of the black car, and its back panel crumpled, denting in with the sharp sound of bending metal.

Elena dashed towards the blur, her long white nightgown blowing against her legs. Maybe there was still time. The lot was full, but no one else had seen, their eyes fixed on the movie.

Above her on the screen, Mina Harker was saying, 'I felt its breath on my face and then my lips . . .' and then gasped. There was no sign of Siobhan anywhere. The trail of her aura had vanished.

Elena turned back to the car. Two figures were silhouetted in the front seat, leaning together. As Elena got closer, she could see long dark hair, the girl's face pressed close against the neck of the guy. It almost looked like another feeding vampire, but they were too still. Maybe they were just unconscious, but dread pooled in Elena's stomach.

She reached for the passenger door of the car and yanked it open.

When the door opened, the couple slumped sideways

like rag dolls, any illusion of life disappearing. The girl's arm flopped limply over the seat on to the floor of the car. Her neck was destroyed. The guy's cheek rested upon hers and he gazed vacantly past Elena, his eyes empty. Tentatively, Elena reached out and touched the guy's neck, then felt the girl's wrist for a pulse. They were both dead, but their skin was still warm, their blood still wet.

Elena's heart pounded, blood rushing dizzyingly in her ears. She had been just a few moments too late.

On the flickering black-and-white screen above Elena's head, Mina, her voice full of horror, was telling the vampire hunter Van Helsing, 'She looked like a hungry animal . . . a wolf. And then she turned and ran back into the dark.'

Elena turned the steering wheel and noticed, with a shiver of disgust, that there was a smudge of blood on the back of her hand. Pulling a tissue out of her glove compartment, she wiped it away.

In the end, she'd left Siobhan's victims where she found them. Everyone in the audience had their eyes fixed on the screen above them; no one had seen her. It hurt to abandon them like that – their broken bodies gazing glassily at her, as if silently asking for some kind of acknowledgment – but getting tied into a police case would cause complications.

Once, finding two dead bodies would have horrified

and traumatised Elena. The girl she used to be would have called the police, would have wept. She'd seen so much since then. Now all she could muster up was pity and a hard determination to catch Siobhan, to stop her. Elena didn't know when she had become this colder, tougher person.

Before she could really think about it, about how she had changed, she caught a flicker of a peacock-blue and rust-red aura in the woods to the side of the highway. Damon. Their bond tugged insistently in her chest, and she pulled over.

She could feel him coming towards her, and a moment later the passenger side door opened and Damon climbed into the car. He was smiling, and Elena felt a sharp pull of excitement, not her own. Damon was up to something. She found herself smiling back at him, her heart lifting.

'What's going on?' she asked.

'I could ask you the same question. You're a little underdressed.' Damon said, his gaze skating curiously across her lacy nightgown. Then he stiffened. 'Are you bleeding?'

'What?' Elena said, and realised. 'No, not me. I got a Guardian task and I wasn't . . . I didn't find the vampire, but I found some victims.'

'Jack's your task?' Through the bond, she could feel his pleasure that the Guardians might finally be on their side.

Elena sighed. 'No,' she said. 'A different vampire, a real one.'

'Don't let this distract you,' Damon said quickly. His voice was flat, but there was urgency underneath it, and pain. 'Jack's the most important thing. For Stefan.'

'Damon . . .' she said, reaching for his hand.

There was a cracking noise like a gunshot, and the roof of the car suddenly dented in. Elena screamed as a figure leapt from the roof of the car, kicking in the window. Damon was outside in a flash, blue squares of safety glass scattering everywhere.

Elena barely had time to draw a shocked breath when Damon ripped the back door of the car open and shoved in a struggling figure dressed in black. *A vampire*, she realised. One thin-fingered hand flailed out and caught Elena's hair, dragging her head back against the seat. She shrieked as sharp pain shot through her scalp, and then again as Damon jerked the vampire's arm back, long strands of Elena's hair still dangling from its fingers.

'Don't touch her!' Damon hissed, throwing himself on top of the other vampire and clamping one heavy hand on the back of its neck. Elena could feel Damon's vicious satisfaction in the violence, his pleasure in being able to act, to win against an enemy again.

'What are you doing?' Elena asked, pressing a hand against her aching scalp as she twisted around in the driver's seat to get a better look. The vampire was young, looked younger than she was. He writhed and growled as Damon shoved his face down against the seat and hit him hard between the shoulder blades. Finally, he grew still, trapped beneath Damon and panting hard. His dark eyes were fixed on Elena, his face distorted with hatred and fury. He bared his teeth at her, his canines long and sharp. If he managed to get loose . . .

It must be one of Jack's synthetic vampires, she realised, because his aura seemed just like a human's.

'I can tell now,' Damon said breathlessly, picking up on her curiosity. 'There's a touch of something *wrong* about them. I don't know what exactly. It's like a chemical taint.' The vampire bucked under him and Damon hit him on the back of the head, forcing out a grunt of pain. 'He was lurking outside our building. He thought he could get to us.'

Elena's stomach lurched.

Picking up on her fear, Damon wrapped a hand around the younger vampire's throat, squeezing. *See how much stronger I am than he is*, his face seemed to say. *I'll protect us.*

'Don't kill him in my car, Damon,' Elena objected, her eyes drawn back to the young vampire's furious face.

'I can't kill him. I don't know how,' Damon said, but he was grinning. The vampire growled, the sound muffled against the backseat, and Damon smacked him lightly on the back of the head, his other hand still tight around his throat. 'I'm going to do some research. Where can we keep him?'

'Not the apartment, that won't hold him,' Elena said quickly. 'Let me think.'

'Somewhere no one will overhear,' Damon said. 'Somewhere we can keep him under control.'

Elena started the engine and pulled out on the highway, heading for campus. 'My old dorm. It'll be empty for a few more weeks, and there are storage rooms, like cages, in the basement.' Damon looked doubtful, and she added quickly, 'They're strong. And no one will hear him down there.'

'Excellent,' Damon said, and Elena felt another flare of excitement from him. 'There's something I want to try.'

CHAPTER

9

Meredith dug her nails into the palms of her hands and tried not to breathe. The vampire – the young vampire; he looked like a high school kid – was watching her, leaning against the bars of his cage. Beneath his shaggy black bangs, his dark eyes shone with hate. Both of his wrists were chained to the steel bars of one of the dorm's basement storage cages, and he twisted his wrists against them unceasingly, testing the handcuffs for weakness. Damon must have found a way to weaken him, so the chains were enough to hold him.

Damon tapped the bars between them, poking at the vampire's face, and the kid lunged, snapping at him with sharp teeth. Damon pulled his hand back with a laugh. 'You see, he's fast, but no faster than I am,' he told them. 'I wanted to show him to you all, because I want your help in figuring out how Jack made him, and how to kill him.'

The trapped vampire was growling, softly but steadily, like a savage animal. The sound grated on Meredith's nerves, and when Alaric's hand brushed against her arm, she jerked away.

'Are you OK?' he asked her quietly, and she nodded, not looking at him.

'I'm fine.' She had to keep her distance from Alaric. She felt sick, thinking about it, but she could still smell the tantalising, salty scent of his blood.

'It's so creepy, the way he's just staring at us,' Bonnie said. Her small face was wrinkled with disgust, and she clung to Zander's arm. With a jolt, Meredith realised she was the only one who could hear the vampire's growling.

Meredith felt dizzy. She was just like this kid huddled against the bars. What would Elena say if she knew what Meredith was now? Or Bonnie? Would they want to chain her up the same way?

Damon knew about her, but Damon was practical: he thought Meredith was his best route to finding Jack. Not to mention that he'd given his word, and Meredith knew that once he gave it, Damon never broke his word. Besides, she'd find a cure before anyone else found out the truth, she promised herself, stuffing her hands into her pockets so no one could see them shake.

Behind her, Jasmine pressed her back against

the wall, as far from the imprisoned vampire as she could get. She was holding tightly to Matt's hand, and Meredith could hear her quick, panicked little breaths. This was Jasmine's first face-to-face encounter with an unfriendly vampire, Meredith realised. Matt was stroking her hair with his other hand, comforting, his attention on Jasmine. The vampire thrashed and kicked, straining against his bonds, the handcuffs clanging against the bars of his cage, and Jasmine yelped, burying her face in Matt's shoulder.

'Let me try something,' Damon said, and picked up a stake from the floor. The vampire in the cage stopped twisting at his handcuffs and stood very still, his eyes narrowed.

'We know that won't kill him,' Elena said, her voice even. She and Damon glanced at each other, clearly in perfect accord. They were strangely alike, Meredith thought.

'It'll hurt, though,' Damon said cheerfully. Turning, he slammed the stake between the bars and into the vampire's chest. The kid gasped, a long rattling breath, and his eyes flew wide open. Damon pulled the stake out. A bright bubble of blood swelled out of the wound and trickled down the vampire's chest, but Meredith could already see the hole closing up, leaving the vampire's chest unmarked.

'You see how quickly he heals,' Damon told them.

Meredith flinched. The kid probably hadn't asked for

71

this to happen to him, either. That was true of most vampires, she supposed. They'd all been victims once. It wasn't something she'd worried about, until now.

She pulled her hand from her pocket and rubbed at her forehead. It was too much – the noise and the smells of her friends' blood, all of them crowded together down here – and she was so hungry. She hadn't had any blood since that shameful night Damon had found her.

'Want to tell us where Jack's hiding?' Damon said, his voice friendly. Meredith glanced between Damon and Elena. Elena was nibbling on her lip, her eyes bright. This was about Stefan, of course. It wasn't just a vampire hunt. If they couldn't take vengeance on Jack directly, torturing one of his creations would help.

The vampire bared his teeth at Damon. 'I don't need to tell you,' he said. He sounded sulky, like the human teenager he had been probably only a month or two before. 'Jack'll find you, and then you'll be sorry. I hope he lets me help kill you.'

'Wrong answer.' Damon shoved the stake through his chest again, and the kid screamed, a high shrill sound. Meredith shuddered.

When Damon pulled the stake out with a sickening squelch, the kid hung against the bars for a moment, panting, before the sullen expression settled back on his face. 'He'll get me out,' he muttered, and his eyes fixed on Meredith's. Frozen to the spot, she met his gaze. Did he know what she was?

Damon grinned, an angry, deadly grin, and gripped the stake again.

Alaric coughed. 'Instructive as this is,' he said dryly, 'weren't we going to discuss our plans?'

'Right.' Damon loosened his grip on the stake and turned away from the young vampire.

In that second, the vampire lunged at him with teeth and clawed fingers, reaching through the bars between them, moving so fast Meredith's eyes could barely follow. Without thinking, she charged forward, shoving the kid away, her hands slamming against the bars of his cage.

'Thank you.' Damon stepped back, rubbing at his neck. He glanced at the trapped vampire, his eyes sharp. 'We'll talk about this later,' he said, his tone threatening. The kid hadn't been able to reach far, bound as he was, but there were bloody scrapes across the side of Damon's throat.

Relief loosened Meredith's chest and she took a deep breath. When it had come down to it, she was still on the right side. All this hunger she was feeling, the way all her friends, except Damon, smelled like food, was just a technicality. She was going to be fine.

'Damon found this vampire outside our building,' Elena told them all. 'We have to assume it means that Jack knows that Damon's living there and will send more vampires after him. He's on Jack's list, and we all know how far Jack will go to . . . eliminate his enemies.' She sounded businesslike, but Meredith could hear the undercurrent of fear in her voice. Elena couldn't handle losing anyone else.

'So we need to step up our game,' Bonnie said cheerfully. 'I'll pull out all the tracking spells I can think of, and make some more protection charms for all of us. Zander and the Pack can—'

'Uh.' Zander broke in, looking uncomfortable. 'We've got a lot of official Pack business going on right now. I mean, I'll do whatever I can, but I don't think you can count on the whole Pack.'

'But . . .' Bonnie looked confused.

Zander shifted from one foot to the other, his white-blond hair falling into his eyes. 'We'll patrol like we usually do, I just don't know how much else the guys are up for.' He wasn't looking at Bonnie, or at any of them.

Meredith frowned. Zander was acting peculiar. Then she caught a full whiff of Zander's scent as he moved, and couldn't think of anything else. His blood would be strong and wild, she knew, and she couldn't help imagining how an alpha werewolf might taste. Her teeth ached, and she stepped back away from him. Clearly, she wasn't fine yet. She had to fix this.

Damon's eyes met hers for a moment, and she was surprised by the sympathy in his gaze.

'OK,' Elena said briskly. 'Bonnie, that sounds great, and Zander, just have the Pack do what they can.' Zander nodded. Bonnie was still staring at him, her lips slightly parted.

'You and I will work on this fellow,' Damon said to Elena, with a vicious glance at the trapped vampire, who snarled back at him. 'If we can't get information on Jack out of him, maybe we'll be able to figure out how to kill him.'

'If I can get some of his blood, I can analyse it at the hospital to see how Jack is making his vampires,' Jasmine offered shyly. 'Maybe Matt can help me.'

'And I'd like to try to track down Jack's history,' Alaric added. 'The more we learn about who he was before he became a vampire, the better we'll be able to fight him.'

From behind Alaric, Damon caught Meredith's eye and cocked an eyebrow at her. They'd already discussed Meredith's next step.

'I want to head down to Atlanta for a while, talk to Darlene and the other hunters who were working with Jack,' she said, slipping easily into the lie they'd decided on. 'They've got to know something they haven't told us, something that will help us track him.'

Alaric took a half step towards her, his mouth opening in a question. Of course he was surprised – she hadn't discussed this with him at all.

'It's important,' she said, begging him with her eyes

to understand. Alaric bit his lip, and then his face softened. He knew how she had admired Jack, back when she thought he was a hunter, and Meredith could see him deciding that this would be good for her.

'OK,' he said. 'Don't be gone long, though. We should all be sticking together right now.'

Elena frowned. 'You're probably the best one to figure out how to kill this vampire.'

Damon put a hand on Elena's shoulder, and she leaned towards him. 'I can handle the fake vampire,' he said smoothly. 'Meredith should do what she has to do.'

It would be good to get away, Meredith thought. She had to get away before she hurt the people she loved.

She couldn't live like this. Jack must know something. There had to be a way to undo what he had done to her. All she had to do was make him trust her.

Meredith left the next day, amidst a flurry of a send-off. She kissed Alaric, hugged Elena and Bonnie and the others. Damon hung back, watching her with sharp, half-amused eyes. Meredith promised to touch base often, told them she'd let them know when she got to Atlanta. The whole time she concentrated on not breathing, to avoid catching anyone's scent, and managed to keep herself from sinking her teeth into anyone's throat.

Once she had driven a few miles away from home,

Meredith pulled on to the shoulder to take a breath and let herself think.

'We can find out more by infiltrating Jack's group than by capturing him,' Damon had said. 'That's where you come in.'

Licking her lips nervously, she reached into her bag and pulled out the business card she had found in her pocket that first terrible day, now creased and fuzzy at the edges. *I can do this*, she told herself. *I am a hunter. It doesn't matter if I'm afraid, I'll still keep fighting*. Then she pulled out her phone and dialled the number written on the card.

'It's Meredith,' she said when Jack picked up. 'You were right. Please. I have to see you.'

Jack's hideout wasn't far away. Following the directions he'd given her over the phone, Meredith found a road that ended outside a long-abandoned warehouse at the edge of town. She got out of the car, slamming the door behind her, and crunched her way across the gravel parking lot.

The warehouse was dilapidated, and there were no cars in the lot except hers. A fast-food wrapper blew across the ground in front of her. Everything was eerily silent.

It didn't matter. She knew Jack was here.

The warehouse's big metal door rattled when Meredith knocked on it. She could hear footsteps coming. When it opened, there stood Jack, his face carefully neutral.

'Meredith,' he said, a little warily.

'I still hate you,' Meredith said quickly. 'You killed Stefan, and I can't forgive that. But—' She paused, her heart pounding, uncomfortably aware that what she was about to say was only partially a lie. 'I don't belong anywhere else. I can't – all I want to do is bite people. I need to be in a place where my friends are safe from me. I need to be away from them.'

There was a long pause while Jack looked her up and down, his mouth pursed. Meredith shifted uncomfortably under his gaze. Could he tell that she had come to spy on him, that she and Damon were working together?

'Please,' she dropped her voice as if she was telling him a shameful secret. 'You were right. It feels good. I didn't – don't – want to be a vampire, but physically, I feel alive for the first time in my life. I want you to show me what I'm capable of.'

Jack stared at her, his face unreadable. Meredith kept her eyes steady on his, trying to project sincerity and pleading. She needed him to believe her, or she'd lose all chance of finding a cure.

Jack frowned, and for a moment she thought he'd slam the heavy metal door in her face. But then his lips turned up in the warm smile she had loved, back when she thought he was her friend. 'Come on in,' he said. 'We've all been waiting.'

CHAPTER

10

The trapped vampire let out a high, wordless shriek and tried to scrabble away from Damon, his chains clanging against the bars of his cage. Streams of gasoline ran down his legs, leaving long, wet patches on his clothes. Elena gritted her teeth and kept herself from looking away. This was important. This was to avenge Stefan, to save Damon. Besides, she thought wearily, he would be healed again in a matter of seconds.

'Stop fighting,' Damon said, his voice flat. The young vampire kicked at him, but Damon grabbed hold of his leg through the bars and pinned it for a moment as the vampire tried to twist away. 'Hand me the lighter, Elena.'

Holding her breath to keep from inhaling the fumes, Elena reluctantly pulled the lighter from her pocket and handed it over, then backed a few steps away, watching them nervously. Damon flicked it and reached through the bars to touch the flame to the edge of the vampire's pant leg.

The cloth burst into flame immediately and burned fast, green and blue flames flickering off the vampire's body, his skin blackening. He screamed again and kicked free of Damon's restraining hand. Losing his catlike grace for a moment, Damon stumbled back into Elena, knocking her forcefully into the wall.

'Elena!' he cried.

'I'm OK, I think,' she said, rotating her shoulder experimentally. It hurt where she'd hit the wall and her mouth had a coppery taste of blood, but she would be fine.

Damon picked up a fire extinguisher from the floor beside him and sprayed it across the young vampire, quenching the flames. 'Cooperate,' he said again, his voice low and threatening.

'What're you going to do if I don't, set me on fire? That's not working out too well for you so far,' the vampire said, breathing hard. His face was smudged with smoke and his pants were in tatters, but the skin beneath the clothes, which had been blackened a moment before, was already pink and healthy again. 'When I get loose, I'm going to kill you.'

Damon laughed, sounding genuinely amused. 'OK, kid, you do that.'

Scrambling to her feet, Elena grimaced. Their prisoner was glaring at her defiantly, dark eyes in a pale pointed face.

'So fire doesn't work either,' Damon said thoughtfully to her, tapping his fingers against the bars of the cage. 'We're running out of ideas on how to kill him. I fed him rat poison yesterday, but it didn't do a thing.'

Elena felt a twinge of discomfort, and she knew Damon sensed it by the way he tensed in response. 'I'm not sure we should keep torturing him this way, Damon,' Elena said reluctantly. Damon was enjoying this too much. He'd been careless and ruthless, sometimes, but he'd never really struck her as vicious, not before Stefan died.

A warm feeling of affection came through their bond. Damon loved that she wasn't as ruthless as he was, Elena knew. He loved the human side of her. All he said, though, was, 'He'd killed three teenagers that I know of before I caught him, if that's any comfort to you. Friends of his. I buried them to stop from causing a panic.'

The vampire boy, already recovered from the flames, shot Elena a narrow smile and rattled his handcuffs against the bars of his cage. The sound echoed throughout the cavernous empty basement. 'They were delicious,' he said, eyes tracing over the vein on her throat. 'I'd do it again if I had the chance.'

Elena leaned back against the bars of the storage unit

on the other side of the aisle, as far as she could get from the vampire boy's malicious gaze. 'Did you try to influence him?' she asked Damon.

'No use,' Damon replied. 'Watch.'

He leaned in close to the bars and looked into the boy's eyes, his gaze intent. Elena felt the stirring of his Power as he pulled upon it. 'Bite your own wrist,' he said to the boy soothingly. 'Tear it open. It won't hurt.'

For a moment, Elena thought it might work. The young vampire turned his wrists thoughtfully, pulling against the handcuffs. Then the boy's lips curled into a sneer and he spat directly in Damon's face.

'Ugh,' Damon said, pulling back and wiping at his face. 'Nasty little thug. We'll go on seeing how long it takes him to starve then, shall we?' This was said with a sharp glare at the boy.

'What will that prove? It's not like we can starve Jack,' Elena said uneasily. Again, she felt that flash of affection from Damon. He liked when she disagreed with him, liked their verbal sparring. She glanced up to see him watching her, his dark eyes intent. He was sensing her anxiety and trying to make her feel better, she knew, and something in her relaxed. He couldn't be going off the deep end, not if he still wanted to make her happy.

Elena didn't quite know what to do with the warmth of the feelings passing between them. *Stefan*, she thought, and bent her head, hiding her face behind her long fall of hair.

Damon cocked his head, listening to sounds too faint for Elena to hear. 'Finally. They're here.'

It smelled stale and musty in the basement, and Matt's sneakers and Jasmine's boots kicked up little clouds of grey dust as they walked. Jasmine had a black bag full of medical supplies dangling from one hand, and she looked tense and expectant, her lips tight.

'You don't have to do this,' Matt said suddenly. He couldn't lie and say that having a doctor on their side wasn't a big help, but they could figure something else out if they had to. He didn't want to involve Jasmine in this – at least, any more than she was already.

Jasmine shook her head, frowning at him. 'I told you, I'm all in.' Her lips twitched in a small smile. 'Besides, how many doctors get the opportunity to study this kind of physical transformation?'

They rounded the corner into another row of barred storage rooms. Smoke hung in the air, and there were scorch marks on the concrete floor. Damon and Elena were outside the only occupied one, Elena leaning back as far from the locked cage as she could get. Above their heads, a fluorescent light flickered dizzyingly.

'Thank God you're here,' Elena said. 'We really need a new tactic. Just attacking him isn't doing anything.'

As they drew level with the cage, Matt took another

look at the vampire Damon had caught. He seemed like some little high school punk, the kind who, when Matt had been in school, would have had a skateboard and worn a lot of black clothing. 'He doesn't look like he'd be hard to handle.'

Damon stiffened. 'He's stronger than he looks,' he said defensively, and Matt managed to stop himself from rolling his eyes. Damon was so touchy sometimes.

A slow, metallic tapping noise drew his attention back to the young vampire. The kid was staring at Jasmine, clinking his handcuffs steadily against the bars of his cage. As Matt watched, he inhaled deeply and his mouth opened a little, showing his canines, extended and slick with spit. His tongue licked over them briefly, pink against the white of his teeth, and his lips tilted into an unfriendly smile. Instinctively, Matt pulled Jasmine closer.

That reaction came from the part of him that would have kept his caveman ancestors crouching by the fire, he thought, the quick instinctive knowledge that there was something terrible out there in the dark.

'Hold on,' Damon told them. Almost faster than Matt's eyes could follow, he whipped open the door of the cage and dashed inside. The young vampire snarled at him, and there was a brief vicious scuffle. It ended when Damon grabbed his opponent's head with both hands and twisted sharply. There was a loud cracking sound and the kid slumped and slid down the bars, dangling from one chained hand. Jasmine gasped.

'That should keep him down for a little while,' Damon told her. 'Better hurry.'

'He's not dead?' Jasmine asked, stunned.

'That wouldn't even kill me, doctor,' Damon said, amused. 'And he's a lot harder to kill.'

Hesitantly, Jasmine came into the cage and knelt down by the young vampire's side. She felt for a pulse and frowned. 'His heart's beating,' she said, and Damon nodded, backing out of the cage to give her room.

'It'll do that.'

Gaining confidence, Jasmine pulled a syringe from her bag and briskly felt for a vein in the vampire's arm. She drew one vial of blood and started a second. Matt loved watching Jasmine work. Anything nervous or shy about her slipped away immediately. Her hands were deft and quick, her manner calm. It made him feel weirdly proud, that a girl this capable, this self-assured, wanted him.

Jasmine gently moved the kid's arm a bit to help the blood flow. Matt frowned, and took a step forward. Something wasn't right—

With a sudden burst of movement, the vampire's eyes shot open as he flung his arm around Jasmine's neck and yanked her down on to the floor with him. Jasmine screamed shrilly. The vampire wrapped his hand in her curly hair and yanked back her head. Throwing his body half over her, he sank his fangs into her throat, giving a soft sound of pleasure.

'No!' Matt shouted, and charged towards them, his fists clenched.

Damon, moving so fast he seemed like a blur, got there first, yanking the kid away from Jasmine with a snarl of fury. He slammed the young vampire to the ground and snapped his neck again. A trickle of blood ran from the kid's mouth and dripped startlingly red against the dull grey of the concrete floor.

Lifting Jasmine into his arms, Damon dashed out of the cage and slammed the door behind them. She was limp, her head back against Damon's shoulder, eyes closed. Her usually honey-tan skin was grey and drained.

'She's all right,' Damon told them, lowering Jasmine to the floor. Matt reached out and helped, taking Jasmine's weight in his arms. She was sobbing, he realised, her cheeks wet with tears.

'I'm sorry,' he whispered. He knelt down and lowered her head into his lap, her long hair spilling across his thighs. Then he turned to Damon. 'All right?' he said furiously. 'How could you leave her in there with him?'

'His recovery time is getting faster,' Damon said, almost to himself. 'I didn't know.'

I brought her into this, Matt thought, and cupped her cheek gently, feeling sick with guilt. 'I shouldn't have let her go in there,' he said, his voice choked.

Jasmine wiped away the tears, her hands shaking. 'I'm OK,' she said, her voice rough, and tried to sit up.

'Stop!' Matt said, pulling her closer, trying to hold her tight. 'You're bleeding.'

'There are bandages in my bag,' Jasmine said, laying her head back in his lap. Her voice shook, and Matt could see her gritting her teeth, forcing herself to be calm. 'Put pressure on it.'

Elena was already in motion, deftly pressing a cotton pad against Jasmine's neck and wrapping gauze around it. 'The bleeding's almost stopped,' she said. 'It's not as bad as it looked.'

Now that he knew Jasmine would be OK, Matt felt like he was going to throw up. Everyone he had ever fallen in love with had died, even Elena, and he had just gone ahead and let Jasmine into his mess of a life.

'We're going,' he said to her soothingly. 'I'll get you home.' He tried to pick her up again, but Jasmine twisted out of his arms.

'Wait,' she said, determined. 'I want . . . I could use the blood of a natural vampire, for comparison.'

'Jasmine, you don't have to . . .' Matt began, his heart aching.

She gave Damon a shaky smile. 'Put out your arm for me? Please?'

Damon extended one arm, and Jasmine used a fresh hypodermic to draw a vial of blood. She worked efficiently, but as she capped the vial her hands shook and she dropped it, spilling more blood across the concrete floor. 'Sorry, sorry,' she said, her hands fumbling in her bag, a flush stealing across her pale cheeks.

'My fault,' Damon murmured, holding out his arm and smiling reassuringly. 'I'm so clumsy sometimes.'

Matt blinked. Damon Salvatore, gentle and kind with Matt's girlfriend? Bothering to put someone other than Elena at ease?

Matt ran a hand down Jasmine's back, reassuring himself that she was solid and real and not hurt. He was heavily aware of the unconscious vampire, his face turned towards them, soon to awake again.

'You're not safe,' he murmured, almost to himself, and felt Damon's eyes on him. 'None of us are safe, not while Jack and his vampires are after us.'

Part of Matt wanted to rush Jasmine away. If none of them were safe here, wasn't the solution to get away? Jack didn't want Jasmine, didn't want Matt. He was after Damon.

But Matt knew that Elena, whose dark-blue eyes were fixed intently on Damon's face, would never agree to leave him. And he could tell just by looking at Jasmine, capable and strong once more, that she wouldn't either.

'Not until we figure out a way to kill them,' Damon agreed. He nodded to Jasmine. 'That's where you come in.'

Something in Matt hardened. The only thing that mattered was protecting Jasmine.

'You have to keep experimenting on him,' he told Damon, looking at the young face of the vampire in the cage, slack in unconsciousness. 'If we want this to end, we'll have to finish them.'

CHAPTER
11

'More coffee, hon?' The waitress refilled Bonnie's and Elena's cups before moving on to the next table. The little diner halfway between their apartments was busy, bright and cheerful, as it always was on a Sunday morning. They hadn't been here in a while, but Bonnie thought bright and cheerful was exactly what Elena needed right now.

'Sounds like Jasmine's tougher than I thought,' Bonnie said, swiping cream cheese across her bagel. Elena had been filling her in on the latest in the quest to discover the truth about the synthetic vampires. 'Has Meredith found out anything from the hunters down in Atlanta?'

Elena sighed, resting her chin on her fist as she stared into her coffee. 'She hasn't returned any of my calls. I got a text saying she was OK, but that's it.'

'Yeah, same. She's probably busy,' Bonnie offered. Meredith was pretty good at looking after herself. Right now, Bonnie was more concerned about Elena.

Elena had been distant lately, caught up with Damon and with her new Guardian task. Bonnie was glad that she had something to focus on. Elena was still pale and solemn, but she didn't seem as stunned with grief as she'd been right after Stefan's death.

Bonnie ripped open a sugar packet and poured it into her coffee. Mostly to get the sad, distracted expression off Elena's face, she asked, 'How's the search for Siobhan? Any luck?'

Elena scowled. 'I haven't had any leads on her since I lost her aura at that drive-in. I keep dreaming about her, but I can't find her.'

Munching her bagel, Bonnie listened to Elena describe the dreams – a dark-haired woman in a cabin, a blood-red aura, nothing much happening, but a sense of dread overhanging everything – and tried to offer helpful suggestions. 'Maybe she's up in the hills? There's a lot of hunting cabins up there.'

Elena leaned back in the booth, her shoulders slumping. 'I thought of that. I tried walking through the hills, but I didn't feel anything. My Guardian Powers are supposed to lead me to her, I guess I have to trust that they will when the time is right.'

The waitress slapped the check on their table as she

walked by. Bonnie was reaching for it when Elena sat up straighter and frowned at her. 'Anyway,' she said briskly, 'we've talked about my problems, but what's going on with you? You seem stressed.'

'I do?' Bonnie asked reluctantly. She'd been trying to act normal, to make Elena feel better. Elena nodded, and Bonnie rested her temple in her hand. 'I guess . . . Zander's been strange lately. He's always on the phone with the rest of the Pack, but he never tells me what they're talking about. It's like he's got secrets with them that he doesn't want me knowing. He's never been like that before. And then with how weird he was about the Pack not helping defend us all against Jack.' She glanced up at Elena, who nodded in confirmation. 'I can't help wondering –'

As she talked, she thought about how Zander had stayed out late the night before, long past when she had gone to bed, with no explanation, and she could hear her own voice getting higher and softer, like a little girl's, '– wondering if Zander maybe doesn't like me so much any more.'

Elena laughed. 'Listen, Bonnie, if there's one thing I know, it's that Zander's crazy about you. Seriously. You two are perfect together.' Her smile faded, and Bonnie knew she was thinking about Stefan.

'Maybe,' Bonnie said doubtfully, poking her finger through the puddle of coffee left in her saucer. She couldn't really put what she was worrying about into words, and certainly she couldn't explain to Elena, who had not just Stefan but even Damon eternally, endlessly, death-will-not-part-us in love with her. But people did fall out of love, all the time. There was something in Zander's eyes when he looked at her – something sad and faraway. It wasn't the way he used to look at her. 'I'll see him later today, at least. We're going to have lunch and catch a movie.'

'See?' Elena told her. 'Talk to him, and you'll work it out.'

'Maybe,' Bonnie said again. They paid the check and walked out into the bright glare of the sunny parking lot.

Elena hugged Bonnie hard before she got into her car. 'It'll be OK,' she said reassuringly.

Bonnie smiled and raised a hand in farewell as Elena pulled away. Just as she turned to head to her own car, her phone buzzed in her pocket. It was a text from Zander.

Sorry, can't make it for lunch. Catch up with you later. XO

Glaring down at the phone, Bonnie felt her cheeks getting hot. Six years together, and he wouldn't even tell her why he couldn't meet her? He just blew her off?

It was so frustrating. The sunlight dimmed, and she wondered if she was the one doing it. She could feel her Power gathering within her, ready for her to call on nature, work her will. She could ball this Power up and

93

fire it off at Zander, find out once and for all what was going on with him.

Better yet, she could force her Power inside him, make Zander do what she wanted, make him be the sweet, easy-going, loving guy she was used to. She felt energy rising, swirling dark and expectant inside her.

Her heart was pounding like crazy. Bonnie stopped and pressed her hand against her chest, breathing deeply, until the dark energy started to dissipate. What was she thinking? She couldn't use her Power on Zander. It would be using him, abusing him, and if she did that, then she was the one who would kill the love between them.

Stuffing her phone back into her pocket, Bonnie marched over towards her car. She just had to have faith. Whatever was going on, Zander would tell her in his own time.

Meredith crawled through a dark tunnel, the stone cold beneath her hands and knees. Her new vampire vision lit up the rough surface of the tunnel better than a flashlight would have.

She wasn't entirely sure where she was. They'd started out three days ago, she and Jack and his team of synthetic vampires, chasing a band of ordinary vampires through the hills and valleys outside a small town in the Appalachians. But they must have covered hundreds of miles since then. These vampires were wily and experienced, and they'd managed to evade their pursuers for a long time.

But now she and the others had tracked them down at last. Desperate, the vampires had taken refuge from the daylight in a system of caves that honeycombed the hills. It was the perfect time for Jack's synthetic vampires to move in for the kill.

Ahead of her, a boot scraped softly against rock. Meredith's body flooded with adrenalin. She was so close, she could feel it. This hunt was almost over.

She could see the end of the tunnel now, her sharp night vision illuminating where it opened out into the cave ahead. Her hand slipped on a stone, and Meredith froze, listening. Another sound: a tiny shuffling noise, her prey flattening himself to one side of the tunnel exit. She could hear a slow heartbeat, smell the cold scent of a vampire – so unlike the scent of humans.

Her new senses were an advantage here, not a distraction. She was using the meditation techniques they all practised every night, breathing deep and counting slowly to focus her mind and shield her presence. The vampire at the other end of the tunnel stood out like a beacon to Meredith, but if she were doing everything right, and she managed to keep quiet, he would have no idea she was coming.

Pushing off with her legs, Meredith burst from the tunnel like a rocket. With a quick sidesweep of her leg, she took the vampire, an older man with scraggly blond hair, to the ground before he could even react. His mouth dropped open in surprise as he hit the cave floor. She could see so well, see the frown that creased his forehead and the tension in his muscles as he pushed himself back up. He wasn't used to fighting someone stronger than he was, she could tell.

In a second he was charging at Meredith. He slammed into her hard, his cool breath coming in fast little puffs. There was a swift stinging pain in her side, and her eyes filled with tears as she saw the shard of rock he'd used to cut her clutched in his hand. Blinking the tears away, she swung at him, slamming him back against the wall of the cave. His eyes widened, and she knew he had seen the long cut on her side heal itself already.

He stumbled, surprised, and then came at her with renewed, desperate vigour. She kicked at him, but he managed to trap her leg between his thighs, and they both fell, their legs tangled together.

Meredith's head hit the rocks hard, but she immediately started kicking and punching at the vampire above her. Jack chose to hunt the oldest, strongest vampires he could find, the ones who were the real competition for his creations. If this one managed to get away, it would be hard to find him again. He might escape entirely, the way Damon had.

Not that she cared about Jack's plan, Meredith reminded herself fiercely. But no matter what had happened to her, she was still a hunter, and she would hunt. Vampires were still the enemy. From her prone position, she slammed a heel into the back of the vampire's knee, and he staggered.

Adam, another of Jack's team, burst through the tunnel entrance. Charging forward, he drove a stake through the older vampire's chest. With one long gasp, the vampire fell like a stone.

Meredith lay still for a moment and caught her breath. 'Thanks.' She shoved the body off of her and on to the floor. Climbing to her feet, she wiped the older vampire's lukewarm blood off her arms.

Adam, who was young and cute and blond, with a tiny spray of freckles across his cheeks, ducked his head and grinned at her, swiping a hand across the blood smeared on his chin.

'Want a hand getting him out?' he asked.

Together, they pulled the older vampire's corpse through the tunnel. Once outside, they dropped it on top of the pile of bodies the others had brought out. Meredith counted quickly and found all four there. That was it, the whole group they'd been chasing. She felt a bitter satisfaction: she might be wrong, might be different now, but she could still kill monsters, still make the world safer.

'Go, us,' Adam said, pumping his fist, and Meredith found herself smiling at him.

For a minute, it felt like they were what Meredith had always wanted: a real team. There were five of them, not including Jack, all young, fast and strong. Meredith could have liked them, would have liked them, if they were true hunters.

But that wasn't quite what this was.

She was a spy, she reminded herself. She wasn't really one of them. She would never be one of them, she promised herself, not even if she never found the cure.

'Good work, everybody,' Jack said, as he looked over the heap of bodies.

Adam and the others gazed at him in adoration, their eyes wide and shining, and Meredith felt ill. Even if she found a cure for what Jack had done to them all, the others were already lost. They loved Jack. They loved what they'd become. Sadie picked up a blood bag and sipped from it, faked a kick at Conrad, her leg moving so fast it blurred, and they both laughed.

The hunt over, Adam picked up a can of gasoline and began to pour it over the bodies. They'd burn them to make sure they were dead, and to keep curious humans from stumbling across a pile of corpses. Sadie and Conrad, hand in hand, wandered a little further into the woods. Meredith was heading over to offer Adam her help when she saw Jack lead Nick further downhill, holding tightly to his arm as if Nick might try to get away.

There was something furtive about them, and Meredith changed course to follow. She walked quietly, keeping her shield up as Jack had taught her. *Breathe. Count. Hide your aura.* They didn't glance back at her, but she was careful to keep in the shelter of the trees anyway. Her mouth dry and her heart pounding, she squeezed her hands anxiously into fists. Surely, now that she'd been changed, her palms shouldn't sweat.

When they were far enough away from the caves that even a vampire shouldn't have been able to eavesdrop, Jack and Nick stopped and began to talk, their voices low and their heads together. Edging to the other side of a nearby oak tree, her hands on its rough bark, Meredith stopped, too, and held her breath, listening hard.

She couldn't hear what they were saying at first – their voices were too low. She gritted her teeth, frustrated. Did she dare risk getting closer?

But then Jack's voice rose, furious. 'What do you mean, you haven't found her?' he said. His face reddened, and with a quick, violent movement, he shoved Nick against a tree. Lanky Nick ducked back, twisting his body away from his leader.

'I t-tried,' he said, his voice shaking. 'I'm not giving up.'

'She's got to be near here,' Jack said, his tone dark. He leaned into Nick's face, spitting the words at him. 'Try harder.'

Letting go of Nick, Jack turned away. Then, efficiently and viciously, he snatched a tree branch from the ground beside them and, in one smooth, quick movement, jammed it through Nick's chest. Nick screamed, an agonized wail of pain, and lurched away, clawing at the branch.

Meredith couldn't hold back her gasp of horror. *It'll heal*, she reminded herself, clapping her hand over her mouth.

Too late. Jack swung around, looking up the hill. 'Meredith?' he called.

No. Her body tensed to run, but he knew she was there.

Meredith took a deep breath, smoothed her hair, and stepped out from behind the tree. 'Hi,' she said, careful to keep her face cheerful and her voice light and unconcerned. 'Um, we need your lighter. To burn the bodies.'

Behind Jack, Nick strained to pull the branch from his chest, giving a painful-sounding groan as it slowly slid out. 'Nick?' Meredith asked, trying to sound confused. 'Are you OK?'

'Yeah,' Nick breathed, his eyes glassy. He wiped the sweat and tears from his face. The wound in his chest was already closing, but his shirt was stained with blood, and his voice hitched as if he was barely holding back a sob.

'Nick and I had a disagreement. I overreacted,' Jack said slowly. He was looking at Meredith with a speculative expression, and her stomach turned over nervously.

Digging in his pocket, he walked towards her. His eyes were fixed on her, curiously blank, and Meredith steeled herself, trying not to flinch backward.

When he was a few steps away, he stopped and held out a small silver object. His lighter. 'Here you go.' When Meredith looked up at him, he smiled.

She forced her body to relax, and smiled back at him. Maybe he had bought her excuse. She would have to be more careful now, though, in case he was suspicious. That had been too close.

And who was the "she" Jack had been searching for? Meredith's heart sped up, and she took a steadying breath, willing her pulse back to normal.

Jack had a secret. No matter what it took, she would find out what it was.

CHAPTER
12

Matt cleared his throat and looked up at the clock on the wall of the ER waiting room, shuffling his feet with impatience.

The air seemed suffused with a combination of boredom and despair. People sat huddled together, pressing ice or bandages to themselves, or filling out paperwork with exhausted expressions on their faces. In the chair closest to Matt, a tired-looking older man held a cup of coffee with both hands as he leaned forward tensely, his gaze fixed on the door of one of the examination rooms. Matt looked away, shifting from one foot to the other, embarrassed by the naked fear in the man's eyes.

Still, that man would be helped here. They all would. That's what Jasmine did – she helped people. In that way, she'd always been one of them. They fought monsters to protect the innocent, and Jasmine fixed the innocent.

It was such an unequivocally good thing to do – no shades of grey, no occasionally evil vampire allies, no icy Guardians – that Matt's heart swelled with love for her. Jasmine, with her sweet, soft lips and her shining intelligent eyes, was good all the way through. And she loved him, too, despite everything he had seen and done.

Matt leaned back against the vending machine, looking at the elevators. Soon she'd be here. His heart fluttered in his chest at the thought that any minute now, those elevator doors would open and he'd see Jasmine.

His phone vibrated, and he took it out to see a text from Jasmine: *Come up to room 413. There's something I want to show you.*

Matt rode the elevator up to the fourth floor, found room 413 and tapped lightly on the closed door. It immediately jerked open and Jasmine smiled up at him, almost bouncing with excitement.

'Come on in,' she urged, tugging him by the arm. She yanked him inside and closed the door behind them, then leaned against it, grinning.

'What's going on?' Matt asked, looking around. This was obviously some sort of lab, full of shiny white-and-chrome equipment, none of which gave him the faintest clue to its purpose.

'Look at this,' Jasmine said. Leading the way across the room, she hopped up on a stool in front of one of the machines. She turned on a screen and began adjusting dials, her fingers moving competently over the controls. Two complicated-looking graphs showed up on the screen, one above the other.

'I have no idea what you're showing me,' Matt said, staring at the screen.

'I ran an analysis of the two samples of blood I took,' Jasmine told him. 'This is basically a genetic breakdown of Damon's blood –' she pointed at the upper graph '– and this is the man-made vampire's blood.' She indicated the lower graph. 'They're ridiculously similar. Much more similar than either is to normal human blood.'

'I still don't know what that means,' Matt said apologetically.

'Long story short?' Jasmine arched an eyebrow, a pleased little smile on her lips. 'Jack may have made his vampires in a lab, but he didn't do it without help. There are all kinds of chemical and genetic modifications going on here,' she said, pointing to one edge of the lower graph. 'But the basic structure of the blood shows that Jack didn't start with just ordinary human blood. He used real vampire blood. That's not in the lab notes Damon stole from him, but it's definitely true. There was a first step he didn't document in that notebook.'

'Wow.' Matt ran his eyes across the screen as Jasmine

explained her conclusions in more detail. They still meant nothing to him, but he believed she knew what she was talking about. 'It's amazing that you figured this out.' He hesitated. 'Is it going to help us kill them?'

Jasmine's face fell. 'I don't know,' she said. 'The mutated strands must be what keep them from being vulnerable to the things vampires usually die from. But I can't – I'm not a geneticist.'

Seeing the disappointment in her eyes, Matt felt like a jerk. 'This is great, though,' he said hastily. 'The more we know about what Jack's doing, the better.'

He was glad to see Jasmine's lips tilt up again into a smile. And it was true. He had to believe that every bit of information they could scrape up about Jack and his vampires would bring them closer to killing him.

Raccoon, Damon thought, scraping his tongue against his teeth, *is even more disgusting than rabbit.* That was a fact he could happily have gone without ever knowing. He sighed and leaned back against a birch tree, looking up through branches at the stars, so clear and distant. The night forest was quiet around him.

He should just discreetly find a girl who would let him feed on her, as he had in his travels, but somehow he couldn't with Elena around. Even though he hadn't tasted her blood since after the fight with Jack, it didn't seem right to find another companion. Hence the unpleasantly furry entrées.

How had Stefan managed it, decade after decade, resigning himself to the blood of deer and doves and other woodland rabble? Damon bit his lip and then consciously relaxed, lounging against the tree, pushing the thought away. He wasn't going to think about Stefan.

Instead, he reached for his connection with Elena. It was better to think of her, of her soft skin and shining eyes, of her proud spirit and sharp, fierce mind, than to poke again and again at the painful scars left by Stefan's loss.

Her grief was still there, haunting the bond between them. It would never leave her, he supposed, never leave either of them completely. But there was something else there, he thought, something gentler and warmer creeping into her emotions. He thought – hoped – that perhaps it was the way she felt about him.

Licking his lips, Damon let the blood flowing inside him – disgusting, but full of the energy of life – warm him and quicken his Power. Elena thought Siobhan might be in one of the hunting cabins up here in the hills. So Damon was looking.

It probably wasn't what the Guardians wanted, as they'd assigned Elena the task of finding and killing the old vampire, but who cared what they wanted? Dead was dead, and he didn't like the idea of Elena following auras by herself, finding corpses in the night. She was strong, he knew, but she was still so young.

And he was ready to take someone down. His experiments in killing the synthetic vampires were at a standstill. Nothing worked, and his prisoner had taken to staring silently at Damon with dull, resentful eyes instead of fighting back. Restlessly, Damon touched his tongue to his sharp canines. He needed to do something.

He pushed his Power outward, searching, categorising what he found. There was life all around him. Small animals scurried in the undergrowth, an owl swooped overhead. He felt the quick nervous mind of a deer a few yards away and, further on, a family of black bears searching for food. Humans down in the town below, sleeping or indoors. One walking a dog at the edge of the forest.

Nothing other. No vampire consciousness stirring. If Siobhan was in a cabin in the woods, it wasn't one of the ones up here in the hills past the edge of town.

Damon looked up at the stars again and thought about whether he should call another animal to him before he went home. He hadn't tried bear yet; maybe it would be less vile. All that fur seemed like it would be a pain to bite through, though, which might be even worse than the raccoon.

Or maybe he should head down into town, find a game of pool or a fight, make a few humans uncomfortable with a brush of his Power.

He had taken one undecided step towards the woods'

edge when something stopped him short. Tensed, he held his breath and listened.

There was the lightest crackle, as if someone were carefully stepping across dry leaves. Suddenly, with a tingling shock of awareness, wrongness crept up on him, the faint chemical wrongness that was now all around.

Jack's vampires. Now that Jack knew Damon was in Dalcrest, they had been tracking him. The little vampire outside his and Elena's home hadn't been there by coincidence. He had been scouting, and only the fact that Damon had captured him had stopped more from coming there. And now they'd found him here, in the forest. If they were able to track him, they would pursue Damon the same way their kind had chased him and Katherine across Europe. Only now he was alone.

Pushing away a flare of panic, Damon stepped backward so that the birch tree was at his back once more. They wouldn't be able to come at him from behind. He stretched his Power, feeling for the shape of their minds. Even using his Power to its fullest extent, he could barely sense them. It was lucky he had just fed, or he might not have sensed them coming at all. There was more than one – maybe as many as eight or nine, the feel of them quiet but, once he'd found them, distinct from one another.

Jack wasn't among them, he thought, nor was Meredith. He knew the feel of those two minds now, and these felt like strangers. Just how many minions had the mad scientist created?

They were coming closer, almost close enough for him to see them. He peered into the darkness, watching for movement. There was a crackle of dry leaves somewhere to his right, but he couldn't spot them, couldn't find exactly where they were coming from. Growling low in his throat with frustration, Damon took one step to the right, glaring off into the tangle of trees.

The first vampire slammed into him from the left, unexpected, knocking him sideways. She was a young blonde girl, no taller than Bonnie and probably a few years younger, and she took advantage of his surprise, going straight for Damon's throat, her white teeth flashing in the starlight.

Damon caught his balance and grabbed a fistful of her thick hair, yanking her head back and away from his throat. With a quick motion, he managed to snap her neck. She fell limply at his feet, her face empty and innocent. It wouldn't keep her down for long, but she'd be out of the fight for the moment.

'Come on then, children,' he said to the dark shapes he knew were just out of his field of vision, taunting them. 'Are you monsters or cowards?' He hesitated and stared out into the darkness, feeling with his Power. Could he feel something now? The faintest shine of a rust-red aura in the night? "Dilly, dilly, ducks, come and be killed,' he shouted wildly, an old nursery song popping into his head as he strained to pinpoint just what it was he was on the verge of sensing.

There. There and there. All around. They were dropping their shields now, he realised; he could feel them coming from all sides, pressing in eagerly. They weren't intimidated by how quickly he'd put down the little blonde. She'd only been an experiment, like poking a snake with a stick to see how fast it moved. A sense of grim satisfaction rose from them.

They weren't afraid of him, and, deep inside, this shook Damon. He'd fought monsters stronger than he was, demons and ancient vampires. But they'd always been cautious, a little wary, respecting him even if they didn't think he was a true threat.

But he didn't know how to kill these vampires, didn't even know how to hurt them properly, not for long. And they knew it.

There were too many of them, and he was alone. So Damon did the only thing he could. Between one blink and another he pulled his Power fiercely around him, feeling his body violently compact. It was almost too much to manage with only animal blood in his veins, but he was determined. There was no way he was going to be ripped apart in the woods with the taste of raccoon still in his mouth.

Just before Jack's vampires burst through the trees at him, Damon leapt into the air, completing the transition as he jumped. In crow form, he flapped his way above the forest.

They had gotten too close to him that time, he realised, tilting his wings to catch the night breeze. And they would never stop coming after him, now that they'd found him again.

He needed to figure out how to kill them for good.

CHAPTER

13

'I wish Damon was here for this,' Elena said, staring at her own reflection in the dark window.

There are a lot of people I wish were here for this, Bonnie thought. Alaric had invited everyone to his apartment, saying he had new information to share. But "everyone" felt like a lot fewer people now than it ever had.

Bonnie pulled two more chairs into place around the table. Doing this made it so clear to her how many people they were missing. They only needed six chairs, maybe five: Bonnie, Elena, Alaric, Matt, and Jasmine. And Damon, if he showed up. Stefan was gone. Meredith was away, and Bonnie hadn't heard from her for quite a while.

Zander and his Pack should have been here, but he was still acting distant, and Bonnie hadn't seen the rest of the Pack for days. She'd texted Zander to come to Elena's, but she hadn't been surprised when he'd given an evasive reply. She didn't know when he'd be home, where he was.

Six chairs. And it looked like the sixth one would be empty.

'Can't you just do your whole soul-bond thing and call Damon here?' Bonnie asked.

Elena finally turned around and looked at her, shrugging. 'He tunes me out most of the time unless it feels like something's wrong.'

'Really?' Bonnie asked, distracted from her angst. She'd always figured that the bond between Elena and Damon made them perfectly attuned to each other at all times, an open connection of love and longing. Which was totally romantic. And just slightly creepy.

'I tune him out, too,' Elena said. 'We'd drive each other crazy otherwise.' She looked a little wistful as she said it.

Alaric came in from the kitchen and handed them each a cup of coffee. 'You won't believe how much I've found,' he said.

Before Bonnie or Elena could say anything, they heard feet clomping up the stairs outside, and Alaric hurried over to open the door. Matt and Jasmine came in, hand in hand. Bonnie's heart gave a twinge of longing. Where was Zander?

'Sorry we're a little late,' Matt said, 'but we have some interesting news for you.'

Jasmine tipped her head up as Alaric kissed her on the cheek in greeting. 'Have you heard anything from Meredith lately?'

'I just talked to her. She's with the hunters, tracking Jack. No leads yet. She'll let us know right away if they find him.' Alaric smiled, still looking excited about his news, but he seemed tired, too. Bonnie wondered if he was having trouble sleeping without Meredith. Zander had been coming to bed later and later, and she found herself tossing and turning until he came. She wasn't used to sleeping alone.

'Where's Zander?' Jasmine asked, as Alaric herded them all towards the table.

'He couldn't come,' Bonnie said, keeping her voice light. Jasmine just nodded, but there must have been something in Bonnie's tone, because Matt glanced up at her sharply.

'So I've been doing some digging into Jack's background,' Alaric said, handing around photocopies of a newspaper article. The article was in English, but from a Swiss paper, dated five years before. The headline read WOMAN'S DEATH RULED ANIMAL ATTACK.

'You think this is Jack killing someone?' Matt asked thoughtfully. 'Look at how they describe it. Her throat was torn open, she was almost completely drained of blood. Definitely a vampire.'

Alaric shook his head. 'Based on the journal Damon found, Jack's only been a vampire for three years,' he told them. 'But look – at the end.' He tapped the last line of the article with one finger. *Lucia di Russo is survived by two sisters and her fiancé, Henrik Goetsch.*

'OK . . .' Bonnie said. 'Is this supposed to mean something? Because I don't get it.'

'Henrik is Jack,' Alaric said, grinning. 'Once I managed to ferret out his real name through missing persons reports, I was able to find out why he turned from scientist to vampire.'

'Pretty impressive detective work,' Matt said.

'So was Jack – Henrik – experimenting on this woman? His own fiancée?' Elena asked, looking horrified.

'I don't think so,' Alaric said. 'We don't have any record of him having interest in vampires before Lucia was killed. I think this is when he discovered they were real.'

'And instead of being horrified, he decided he wanted to be one,' Bonnie remarked, feeling a little sick.

'I wonder . . .' Jasmine said eagerly. Her shining eyes flew to Matt's. 'We know he started it all with real vampire blood.'

Matt explained that Jasmine had used the lab equipment at the hospital to analyse the blood she had drawn from Damon's captive. It was clear that Jack hadn't, after all, just transformed humans into synthetic vampires with drugs and surgery as they'd thought. There had been a real vampire's blood in the mix.

'What if it wasn't just any vampire?' Jasmine asked eagerly. 'What if it was his fiancée's killer?'

'We don't have any proof of that,' Elena said, leaning forward intently, her golden hair swinging forward around her face. 'But whoever it was, he would have needed some kind of relationship with the vampire he got the blood from. Whether he forced them to give him the blood, or if they did it willingly . . .'

Alaric was nodding. 'That vampire would know something about him.'

Matt shifted in his seat and let out a frustrated huff of breath. 'But that doesn't really do us any good, does it? If Jack's going around trying to kill all the regular vampires, probably the first thing he did was kill this one. Even if he didn't, we don't know who the vampire was, and I don't see how we're going to find out.'

Elena raised her head and fixed Bonnie with a shining gaze. 'Bonnie can do it.'

'I can?' Bonnie asked, thrown off balance.

'Sure!' Elena said. 'If we still have the blood, you can do a locator spell. It'll be easy for you, you're so Powerful now.'

Bonnie bit her lip, worried. 'But the blood we have doesn't even belong to the vampire we want to find,' she said. 'It would be like trying to use your own blood to find your grandparents.' Her mind was busy, though.

It might work. Blood was powerful stuff – even human blood had a lot of magic in it. It was life, vitality and connection. If she could follow those connections . . .

'I'd need some of the synthetic vampire blood,' she said dubiously.

'I have that,' Jasmine told her. She dug into her purse and pulled out a small stoppered vial. 'I thought we might need it.'

Bonnie met Elena's eyes, and knew the other girl could see the ideas sparking in her mind.

'OK, then,' Elena said, grinning at her. 'Tell me how we can help.'

Under Bonnie's direction, they cleared the table and dimmed the lights. 'Candles,' Bonnie told them decisively. 'Red ones, if you have them.' Alaric was able to dig up one red candle and three white ones, which they grouped at the centre of the table.

Bonnie headed into Alaric and Meredith's kitchen and puttered around, opening drawers and cabinets, until she found a marble mortar and pestle. She'd left some herbs here, a small stockpile for emergencies, and she dug around in the cabinet under the sink to find them. Ground mastic and juniper berries would help with divination, she thought, and there was some sandalwood oil that couldn't do any harm. Poke root was good for finding lost objects – maybe it was good for looking for vampires, too.

She dumped the herbs into the mortar and poured a

little sandalwood oil over them, then mashed everything together with the pestle. Carrying it back out to the living room, she plunked it down on the table in front of the candles.

Elena handed her a book of matches and Bonnie carefully lit the candles, then reached to take the vial of blood from Jasmine. The blood had coagulated a bit. When she tipped it over above the pile of herbs, it trickled out, leaving a thick film inside the vial.

'Don't use it all,' Elena breathed, hanging over Bonnie's shoulder. 'What if we need to do it again?'

'I don't want to make the herbs too wet, anyway,' Bonnie told her, capping the vial again. 'They need to burn.' She handed the vial, a third of its contents gone, back to Jasmine and reached for another match.

The blood- and oil-drizzled herbs smoked and sputtered, letting out a hissing noise as they slowly began to burn. Bonnie fixed her eyes on the smoke, watching the patterns as it curled before the bright candle flames. She slowed her breathing and let her eyes slip out of focus, a deep calm coming over her.

Riding a surge of Power, Bonnie pushed outward, letting her mind expand. The red trickle of blood from the vial. Blood pounding through veins, drunk by vampires, passing from one vampire to another in an exchange of blood. Jack's hands holding a syringe.

She could feel her eyes rolling back into her head and her mouth filled with a metallic, bitter taste. In the distance, Jasmine gasped and Matt shushed her quickly.

Then it was like Bonnie was speeding through the night sky above Dalcrest, the wind rushing through her hair. She hovered over the campus, feeling the pull towards Pruitt House, her old dorm, where she knew the captive vampire was locked in the basement. *No*, she thought firmly. *Someone else. Further back.*

There was an immediate jerk at her consciousness, but weak and in more than one direction, scattered. *The other vampires Jack made*, she realised. There were a lot of them, more than she'd supposed.

No, she thought again, more firmly. *Further back. Older.*

For a moment, she thought it was hopeless. Her consciousness hovered uncertainly, and then started to slide backward. She could see herself from above, her red head tilted back, the black smoke rising from the mixture of herbs and blood towards the ceiling. She was falling back into her body. *No!* she shrieked silently, trying to pull away.

There was a sudden tug somewhere in her centre, and Bonnie was rising again, flying faster, feeling light and buoyant. She zoomed over the campus, past Pruitt House, past the playing fields, and felt herself slow as she reached the stretch of woods on the other side of campus.

There was something – someone – down there. The blood was yanking her towards it. The sensation was stronger than what she had gotten from the vampires in the woods and somehow felt older and darker than the pull towards Damon's captive.

Down, down, closer and closer. The image was becoming clearer: a shadowy figure in a small room. Some kind of little house deep in the woods behind the campus. Through the window she glimpsed the bell tower of the Dalcrest chapel.

Satisfied, Bonnie let her concentration slip. Immediately, she was rushing backward through blackness, feeling like she was falling, and then her vision cleared. Through the smoke of the burning herbs, thin and wavery now, the candles sputtered. Her friends were all watching her.

Bonnie cleared her throat, her mouth dry. 'I know where the vampire is,' she said. 'And it's close.'

CHAPTER

14

As they walked through the woods, Elena sent her Power questing out around her, trying to find some trace of the vampire Bonnie said was nearby. Nothing. Beside her, Bonnie moved confidently straight ahead, seemingly sure of their direction. The others followed, Alaric muttering a charm of protection, Jasmine holding a stake and Matt a long hunter's stave. The sun was rising over the trees and the birds sang loudly, waking up around them.

Matt cleared his throat. 'I really think we should have waited for Damon before coming out here.' He sounded nervous, and Elena didn't blame him. But they knew where the vampire who'd provided the blood for Jack was, and Elena couldn't just sit back and let this chance slip away. It had been hard enough to wait for daylight. They weren't total idiots – they weren't going to go after a traditional vampire at night.

Every moment before sunrise, though, Elena had felt anxious and jittery, ready to burst out of her skin. If she had been just a few minutes earlier at the drive-in, she could have caught Siobhan, could have saved the lives of that young couple in the car.

If she'd seen through Jack's facade just a few minutes earlier, maybe she could have saved Stefan.

'We can't wait for Damon to get back,' she said, determined. 'This might be our only chance to track it down and find out about Jack.'

Matt's Adam's apple bobbed as he swallowed hard, but then he gave her a small smile and pressed forward. Jasmine's face was set and Bonnie's small chin jutted forward defiantly. Alaric nodded at Elena.

We can do this, she thought. *We* have *to*.

The woods opened up into a clearing with a small house at the centre, and they stopped at the edge, still sheltered by the trees.

'That's it,' Bonnie said.

Hansel and Gretel, Elena thought. It looked just like the witch's cottage, gabled and ornamented with a swooping roof. Scrollwork edging hung off the porch and windows. The cottage was precious and nestled deep in the woods. Elena wiped her sweaty palms on her jeans. There was something about this little house.

'Are we ready?' she asked, staring at the house. Its

windows flashed, reflecting sunlight back at her. Did something move behind them? She tried to focus her Power to see if she could sense an aura there, but felt nothing.

'Maybe we should try talking to the vampire first,' Matt blurted out. They all looked at him, and he blushed. 'He – or she – hasn't attacked us. We want information, not a fight. And we know not every vampire is just going to try to kill you right away. Damon wouldn't. Stefan and Chloe wouldn't have.' Jasmine's hand slipped into his, Elena noted. So Matt had told her about poor Chloe, his college girlfriend who had become a vampire and then died.

'You're right,' Bonnie said. 'I'm not sure how long we'll be able to hold a vampire anyway, without Damon's help.' She glanced at Alaric. 'If we can put a strong enough protection spell over all of us.'

As they spoke, Elena's discomfort was growing, vague twitchiness escalating to apprehension. She began to breathe faster, her heart banging against her chest. She focused on the ground floor windows. They seemed ominous, like hooded unfriendly eyes gazing out at her across the porch.

'There's something wrong,' she said suddenly. She was sure of it.

She had to get in there right now. Something inside her was opening up and she felt hypersensitive to everything around her: the breeze through the trees, the chirp of the birds, the fresh morning smell of pines and maples. Most of all, the tiny house where nothing moved.

It was her Guardian Powers. Behind those blank windows, some innocent human was in trouble.

'What's going on?' Bonnie asked her, but Elena was already striding out into the clearing, abandoning any attempt at stealth. She barely noticed the others hurrying after her.

The porch steps creaked under her feet. Up close, the gingerbread cottage was grimy and out of repair, the scrollwork trim cracked. Elena hesitated for a second, clutching her stake. She tried again to find an aura inside the house, but her perception remained frustratingly blank. The sense that something terrible was happening only grew stronger.

'We have to get in there right now,' she said urgently. She slammed her shoulder against the door once and then again, grunting in frustration when the latch held. 'Help me.'

Matt, stave in hand, took a running leap and kicked the door open. It hit the wall behind it with a crash, bouncing back towards them, and Elena shouldered it aside as she rushed into the cottage.

At first, the room seemed empty. The sun shone peacefully through the windows, falling on an empty sofa, a patterned rug. But the smell of blood hung in the air, heavy and overwhelming.

Elena turned – and froze in horror.

For a moment, she wasn't sure what she saw. There was just a pattern of reds and flesh tones against the white wall.

As Elena's vision cleared, the abstract blood-red shapes resolved to a hanging figure. A young girl, maybe fourteen years old, chained to the wall. She had been torn open, bright blood everywhere. Dark, glazed eyes stared unseeingly from a bloody face. Her hair was a honey shade of brown. Elena's heart twisted with pity. She must have been a pretty girl, once.

Elena reached out and ran a hand lightly across the girl's brow, as gently as if the girl could feel it. As if gentleness would do any good now, Elena thought bitterly, and bit her own lip hard to keep from crying. The girl was still warm, but her blood was sticky, drying. Once again, Elena was too late.

'Let me see.' Jasmine pushed in next to Elena, her strong, sure hands running over the girl's body. Pulling off the ropes, she got her down from the wall and started CPR, but Elena knew it was useless. After a few minutes, Jasmine stopped and knelt back away from the body. 'He ripped her apart,' she said, her voice low with shock. 'This wasn't just for food. Whatever happened . . . he wanted to hurt her.'

Matt frowned. 'Forget about talking to him. We'd better go back to planning an attack.'

Elena looked around the room. Blue curtains. Log

walls, wooden floor. A stone fireplace at one side of the room, cold now but blackened with the smoke of an earlier fire. It was so familiar. *Not Hansel and Gretel, but Snow White.*

'Not him,' she told them, her voice a harsh whisper. 'The vampire's a her. Jack's original vampire is Siobhan. My Guardian task.'

It was late afternoon when Damon landed on the sill of Elena's bedroom window. He balanced carefully on the slightly too-small ledge, his talons digging into the wood, and tapped hard with his beak on the window. Elena was in there, he could feel her, and he was too tired to wait.

The Power animal blood gave him didn't last as long as he'd hoped, not as long as a *real* meal. He could have flown for longer on human blood, but now his wings were aching and he felt dizzy and sick. He hadn't wanted to change back while he was out, in case another attack came. He wasn't confident he would have the Power to turn into a crow again.

Elena's quick steps crossed the room and she yanked the window open. 'Damon,' she said.

He fluttered through the window, brushing her face with his longest wing feather as he passed, and landed on the wide soft bed before letting himself transform back into his real shape. Stretching out on Elena's smooth white sheets, he rested his head on her pillow.

Elena's face softened with surprise. 'You're as pale as a ghost,' she said. 'Where have you been?'

Damon sighed. 'The fake vampires found me. I didn't want to come back here until I was sure I'd gotten rid of them.' Elena inhaled sharply, but Damon, closing his eyes, didn't elaborate. He wasn't sure if the false vampires had been tracking him, or if there were just a lot of them around, but whenever he'd been tempted to land, he had felt that strange metallic wrongness. Damon relaxed into the bed, rolling his shoulders back; he was terribly tired.

'Are you all right?' The mattress shifted as Elena sat down on the bed next to him. After a moment, her hand stroked softly over Damon's arm. 'You need blood,' Elena said firmly, and Damon opened his eyes to peer at her.

This still felt like something he shouldn't be allowed to do, not with Stefan dead. But Elena scooted closer and lay down beside him, pushing her silky blonde hair back to expose the long creamy line of her throat. Damon didn't have it in him to resist her offer. Pulling her closer, he moulded his body around Elena's. He could feel his canines lengthening, aching with anticipation, and he kissed her neck gently before he laid the tips of his teeth against it. His canines were so sensitive that he shuddered with pleasure as they touched her.

Elena made a soft, encouraging sound, and Damon

bit down. For a moment, her skin was taut against his teeth, and then they plunged through, blood bursting rich and hot into his mouth.

With the blood came a rush of emotions: love, worry, guilt. Relief at being able to do something for Damon. Under everything, that same constant pounding grief for Stefan.

She was sensing Damon's emotions in return, he knew. He stroked her arm, sending her all the reassurance he could: he was fine, more than fine when he was with her like this. Sometimes he thought all he needed was this, was Elena and his connection to her. He let himself rest against her, felt his lips curve into a smile against the skin of her neck. *Elena Elena Elena*.

And then, unbidden, Meredith's face swam up behind his eyes, and Elena twitched beneath his lips. He was usually better at shielding his thoughts than that; he'd had centuries of practice. He'd gotten distracted too easily.

Private, Damon thought fiercely, half hissing as he arched away, his teeth almost leaving her throat. He could feel Elena's confusion echoing through her blood and their bond. There was a sudden coldness between them, where there had been only tenderness mere moments ago. She began to pull away, and he tugged her back, close and warm against him, his arm around her.

He had promised Meredith, and now that he'd given

his word, Damon couldn't bring himself to break it. Once a gentleman, always a gentleman, he supposed.

He ran his fingers comfortingly through Elena's silky hair in a silent apology, and worked his canines gently in and out of her throat, encouraging the flow of blood. Letting his mouth fill, he reached for his connection with Elena again. But she was holding back now. There was a strange hollow ache inside him, more than hunger.

As she pulled away from him at last, leaving him sated and warm with new blood, Elena wiped one hand across her neck. Damon's gaze followed her hand as it carelessly smeared a single drop of blood towards her shoulder. When their eyes met again, Damon felt an unexpected pang.

She knew he was hiding something.

CHAPTER

15

Bonnie came down the hall of her apartment building slowly, dragging her feet. She was sure the apartment would be empty, and that she'd be having dinner alone again. She'd given up on expecting Zander to be there.

As she turned the corner towards her own door, she stopped in surprise. There was someone kneeling in the hall outside her apartment, crouching to push something under the door. Bonnie's heart thumped hard, adrenalin zinging through her body, and then she realised who it was.

'Hey, Shay,' she said, coming closer. 'What's up?'

Shay, Zander's second-in-command, looked up, her hands half crumpling the edge of the envelope she had been slipping through the gap beneath their door. 'Oh,' she said. 'Bonnie. I was just leaving Zander a note.' Her fingers scrabbled quickly, pulling the envelope back out from beneath the door. Standing, she stuffed the envelope into her pocket.

'Oh.' *Zander's not home. Just as I expected.* 'I can give it to him.' Bonnie reached out, but Shay stepped back, away from her.

'Never mind,' Shay said. 'I'll tell him when I see him.'

'But—' Bonnie gave up. Shay was already turning, her blonde bob swinging, and walking away down the hall. She gave Bonnie a wave over her shoulder, not looking back.

'See you later, Bonnie.'

'Or not,' Bonnie muttered under her breath, unlocking the door. She tossed her keys on the hall table and kicked off her shoes before wandering towards the kitchen. The apartment felt quiet and still. She would have known right away that Zander once again wasn't home, even if she hadn't run into Shay.

In the dim kitchen, she drank a glass of water, and then absently arranged the flower-shaped magnets on the refrigerator door: red, blue, yellow, orange, red. The largest one held a note against the door.

B: I'll be back late. Z

She glared at the note, and with a frustrated sweep of her hand shoved the magnets so that they made a skittering noise against the smooth white surface of the fridge. Zander's note fell to the floor. The note told her nothing. It was almost worse than if he hadn't left her any message at all.

And Bonnie wanted to talk to him, she needed someone level-headed and laid-back – she needed Zander – to help her figure out what she should do.

When she had used the vampire blood to find Siobhan, it had pulled her along like a whirlwind. Back in high school, when Elena had been trapped by Klaus between life and death, Bonnie had used blood to summon Stefan and Damon back to Fell's Church. Ethan had brought Klaus back to life, and Klaus had brought Katherine, with blood.

Bonnie knew blood was dangerous and full of Power. She wanted her magic to be full of light and energy, something that pulled on the growing, striving parts of nature. *Good* magic, not the shadowy ambiguous Power you found with blood and violence.

Still, though . . .

It was scary. It was a really scary idea, one that made Bonnie a little sick just thinking about it. But she couldn't get it out of her head. Blood magic might be what Elena needed. If she could reach Stefan, talk to him one more time, it might give Elena peace, help to ease the grief she carried.

Bonnie crossed to the sink and ran herself another glass of cold tap water. Gulping it down, she stared at the wall and tried to clear her mind. It would be worth it, she told herself. Blood wasn't evil, after all, and she didn't want to use it for an evil purpose. This was important.

Setting the glass down in the bottom of the sink with a firm thump, Bonnie made up her mind. She pulled her phone out of her pocket and called Elena.

'Listen,' she said when her friend picked up. 'Don't take this the wrong way, but do you have anything with Stefan's blood still on it?'

After she got off the phone with Bonnie, Elena eased the bedroom door open and peeked in. Damon was asleep on the bed, his long black lashes heavy against his luminous pale skin. With his eyes closed and his cheeks still slightly flushed from drinking her blood, he looked surprisingly young.

Walking as quietly as she could, Elena crept through the room and to her closet. Damon shifted but didn't wake as she opened the closet door. He must be exhausted; his reflexes were usually as quick as a cat's. Elena was glad he didn't wake. She didn't want him to see this.

Remember how Ethan brought back Klaus? Bonnie had asked.

Blood. It was all about blood. Feeling oddly breathless, Elena peered past hanging clothes, a pile of shoes, until she saw a crumpled paper grocery bag shoved back into the corner. Her chest tight with sorrow, she picked it up and tiptoed out of the room, clutching the bag against her.

She put the bag gently down in the passenger seat of her car and tried not to look at it until she got to Bonnie's.

When she arrived, she hesitated in the doorway, surprised. Bonnie had used a marker to draw a huge black pentacle across the kitchen table, with strange sigils carefully marked inside. Black candles were placed at each point of the pentacle. A brass bowl full of what looked like herbs and roots sat at its centre. Bonnie stood beside the table, shifting anxiously from one foot to the other, her small face drawn with worry.

'That isn't going to come off,' Elena said numbly. 'You've ruined that table.' For a moment, the old wooden kitchen table felt terribly important.

'I don't care,' Bonnie told her. 'Did you find something?'

Elena handed her the bag. 'I couldn't—' She licked her lips nervously. 'I couldn't bear to throw out Stefan's shirt, or wash it. So I just stuffed it in the back of our closet.'

'Oh.' Bonnie looked down at the bag and then hesitantly opened it and pulled out the black shirt. Elena remembered Stefan wearing the shirt that last night, how soft it had been against her cheek the last time he held her in his arms.

Bonnie's nose wrinkled, and a slight rotting smell wafted across the table. Elena flinched. That smell was

Stefan's blood. It had been long enough now that it was festering.

'You really think you can use the blood to bring him back, the way Ethan brought Klaus back?' she asked, her voice sounding thin and stretched to her own ears.

Bonnie bit her lip. 'I don't think so,' she confessed. 'I don't want you to get your hopes up too high. Ethan had to use the bloodlines of all the vampires Klaus had made – that's why he needed Stefan and Damon, because they were what was left of Katherine's line. But Stefan never made any vampires at all. I do think we can do something, though. Maybe we can bring him back, at least for a little while. Or contact him, if he's out there somewhere.'

'Long enough to say goodbye,' Elena said softly. Tears were forming in her eyes. 'I'd like that.'

'I'll do everything I can.' Bonnie put the shirt down on the table and reached out to squeeze Elena's hand. 'Is it OK if I cut this shirt? Just to get a piece with some blood on it.' Elena nodded, and Bonnie let go of her hand and picked up the shirt again, picking up a pair of silver scissors to snip at it.

Taking a glass of water from the counter, she dunked the cloth into it, and they watched as the water gradually turned a cloudy reddish-brown. Tiny flakes of dried blood floated to the bottom of the glass.

'Now I need some of your blood,' Bonnie said, picking up a black-handled knife from where it lay beside the glass. Elena arched an eyebrow questioningly but held out her arm. The blade stung as Bonnie drew it quickly across Elena's arm. Bonnie held the glass so that a few drops of Elena's blood fell into the water and mixed with Stefan's. They both watched as the bright red of the fresh blood spiralled through the browner liquid.

'OK, don't freak out, but I'm going to put some of this on you,' Bonnie said. Elena nodded. Bonnie dipped her finger in the liquid, and Elena squeezed her eyes shut as Bonnie lifted her finger to Elena's face. The water was cold, and Elena shivered as Bonnie's finger traced lightly over her cheekbones, marking what felt like angular symbols on her forehead and below her eyes.

'We want to call him to you,' Bonnie told her, and Elena opened her eyes again to see Bonnie tracing circles and runes on her own cheeks with the thin mixture of blood and water. When she had finished, she placed the glass on the table and lit the five black candles. Their flickering light highlighted the wet brownish streaks on her cheeks, making her look like some kind of pagan priestess. 'Give me some Power.'

Elena took a deep breath and tried to let her Power expand. Blinking, she could see her own golden aura entwine with the rose-pink of Bonnie's. Then Bonnie began to chant in a language Elena didn't recognise, something Germanic-sounding, and picked up the candle at the peak of the pentacle. Shielding the flame with one hand, she dipped the candle and ignited the mixture of herbs inside the brass bowl.

There must have been some kind of accelerant in with the herbs and roots, Elena thought, because flames shot up immediately, blue and green at their base.

'Koma!' Bonnie said firmly. Her voice rose. 'Hitta heima! Koma hyrggr! Leita Stefan Salvatore!' The flames burned higher, and with her last words she upended the glass over them, dumping out the mixture of blood and water. The flames sizzled and went out, sending up a plume of black smoke.

The shadows in the corners of the room seemed to grow darker. A chill crept up Elena's spine. There was a breathless feeling all around them, as if someone stood just outside their field of vision, waiting to speak.

Stefan? Elena strained her eyes, watching the shadows. Bonnie slipped a cold hand into hers, and they waited. Elena's heart was pounding, and she held her breath.

He was coming closer, she was sure of it. She could feel him, that indefinable, comforting feeling that Stefan was somewhere nearby. It was like coming into a room and knowing he was around the corner, just out of sight. Elena's mouth was dry with anticipation.

Slowly, the feeling faded. After a moment, the room grew brighter again. Somehow, it seemed emptier. Elena took a deep, rough breath, her hands shaking. It hadn't worked, she realised. Whatever had hovered at the edges of the room had departed. Elena swallowed hard. It hadn't worked. Nothing was going to work, she realised, coldness spreading through her. Stefan was gone. Forever.

Bonnie looked at Elena, her eyes wet, and took a great gasp of air, letting go of Elena's hand. 'I'm sorry, Elena,' she said.

Elena sagged against the edge of the table and closed her eyes. She shouldn't have hoped, she knew. But, just for a minute, Stefan had seemed so close. Her eyes burned with tears and one slid from beneath her lids and trickled down her cheek.

Immediately, she felt Bonnie's arms twine around her neck. 'I'm so sorry,' Bonnie whispered, her voice shaking.

'I know,' Elena said, bending to rest her face against the smaller girl's shoulder. 'It's OK. I'm just – ' Her voice broke with a miserable half-laugh. 'I'm so tired of crying all the time.'

Bonnie sighed, and hugged her tighter. 'I know,' she said, her voice thick with tears of her own.

CHAPTER
16

Meredith watched carefully as two of Jack's vampires sparred. After a series of hunts, they were back in the warehouse where she'd first found Jack and joined his team.

'Again,' she said, and they lunged at each other. Jack had asked her to help make them better fighters, and she hoped it meant he was starting to trust her, to depend on her. She was conscious of Jack shadowing her as she walked around the fighters. Even when she wasn't looking at Jack, she was hyperaware of him, a prickling at the back of her neck letting her know that his dark eyes were fixed on her.

Soon, maybe, he'd be ready to tell her his secrets.

Broad-chested, stocky Conrad went in with his fists as she'd expected, telegraphing his moves so obviously that anyone could have seen them from about a hundred miles away. Nick, lanky and alert, blocked each blow easily and repeatedly.

'Stop,' Meredith said. She'd seen enough. Sliding between them, she put a hand on each side of Conrad's face. 'You're looking where you're planning to strike. Keep your eyes on Nick's, and he won't be able to guess your next move so easily. Trust your peripheral vision.'

Nick smirked at Conrad, and she stepped back so she could talk to both of them. 'Neither of you is using your feet at all. You're more agile now, you need to trust that.' She showed them how to do a roundhouse kick and watched as they tried it out, nodding approvingly when Conrad landed a solid blow, sending Nick stumbling backward, and Nick returned a solid kick. 'Good.'

She told them to continue sparring, and watched with satisfaction as Conrad slipped a punch past Nick's blocking – they were learning fast.

Maybe tomorrow the whole group could work with weapons. She'd noticed that Sadie liked to work with a stake or an axe, but she'd have more reach with a stave or machete.

Conrad slammed into Nick, knocking him to the floor. 'Nice, Conrad!' Meredith cheered. 'You took him off guard there.'

'Meredith, walk with me,' Jack said from behind her. 'The rest of you, keep sparring.'

His face was blank, giving nothing away, and Meredith felt a trickle of unease. She followed Jack across the warehouse floor, wondering what he wanted. Was there something wrong with what she was teaching the others?

But when he'd led her to the other side of the warehouse – far enough, Meredith noted, that they had some privacy – Jack grinned. 'You're a natural. I knew you would be.'

Laying a heavy hand on Meredith's shoulder, he looked steadily into her eyes. 'You're ready,' he told her. 'I want you to lead this group of vampires when I leave them. You'll be my lieutenant, my right hand.'

'When you leave them?' Meredith asked. 'Where are you going?' She was careful to keep the panic out of her voice. If Jack left, what good would being with the other vampires do? How could she learn his weaknesses, find the cure for what he'd done to her?

Squeezing her shoulder, Jack smiled. 'I'm going to go on with my research, of course. This – you five – are my youngest group. Once the others are ready to hunt under your leadership, I'll go back to the lab. If we're going to eliminate the older vampires, we'll need larger numbers.'

Meredith nodded. It made sense, she supposed. Tracking and killing the toughest vampires was a difficult job. And, usually, a worthwhile one. If it hadn't been for Stefan's death, and for the fact that Jack's people were just as dangerous to humans as any other vampire, she might have supported them. In a lot of ways, they were hunters, like she had been. Like she was.

Jack let go of her shoulder and tucked his hands into the back pockets of his jeans. 'So, if you're going to be my second-in-command here, you need to prove that I can trust you, Meredith.'

Meredith nodded again. This was what she had been waiting for.

Jack looked at her searchingly. 'Do you know where Damon Salvatore is? I know that Stefan was your friend.'

This is a test. Meredith was sure of it. Jack knew that Damon wasn't in Europe.

But nothing she'd ever said to Jack would make him think she cared for Damon. She tried to think back over any conversations they'd had about the Salvatore brothers, back when she'd thought Jack was a human, and a hunter. Stefan had mattered to her. But, even if she'd fought side by side with Damon, he'd never been her friend.

'I think Elena and Bonnie would have hidden him with the Pack,' she said, her voice steady. It would have been a smart move if it was true, and if Damon would ever agree to be hidden. 'They're strong and hard to kill, and they hate vampires. But they'd protect Damon; they've fought beside him before.'

Jack nodded thoughtfully, rocking back on his heels. 'That's a problem,' he said. 'Any ideas?'

'About getting past the Pack?' Meredith thought. If she really wanted to help him, what would she suggest?

Go after Bonnie. She shuddered at the idea. It would work, probably. Zander and the Pack would trade Damon for Bonnie in a heartbeat. But she wasn't going to make that suggestion, not even to win Jack's trust.

'Most of them can change no matter what the moon's like,' she said instead. 'But some of them need the full moon, and all of them are weaker when there's no moon at all. That'll be the best time to attack them.' It was true, which made it the best kind of lie, and the moon was waxing now. If Jack wanted to go against the Pack for Damon, he'd have to wait. 'I'd lure them out with a false attack and, once the Pack is engaged in battle, go after Damon with another group. They'll protect each other rather than fight for Damon.'

'Interesting,' Jack said. 'That may be useful.' He rubbed a hand across his cheek, his ring rasping against his stubble. Giving her a brief nod, he began to turn away.

'Wait,' Meredith said, her heart thumping. 'I wanted to ask you something.' She focused on slowing her breathing and pulse through meditation, the same way Jack had taught them to shield their true natures from others. She couldn't let Jack guess how important this was to her.

'What's our end game here?' she asked first. 'We kill vampires – regular vampires. Is that all there is to it?'

Jack smiled. 'We're going to kill all of them. And then we won't have any competition.'

'I like the sound of that.' Another lie that's true. The hunter in Meredith beamed approval at the idea of killing all the vampires. 'But what happens then? When all the vampires are dead?'

Jack's smile widened, and one of his eyelids dropped in a slow wink. 'One step at a time, my dear.'

Across the warehouse, there was a scuffle and a shout as Nick got Conrad in a headlock, swinging him around.

'Is there a cure?' Meredith asked, her eyes fixed on the fighters. She kept her voice level, but Jack smirked.

'Do you miss the little human hunter you used to be?' he asked. 'You're better now, Meredith, and you know it.'

'I like to know everything,' Meredith said stolidly, not letting out a flicker of emotion.

Jack shrugged. 'No cure,' he said. 'This is who we are. For ever.'

He might be lying. Meredith swallowed hard. 'Is it true that we're invulnerable?' she asked, trying to sound calm and businesslike. 'There's no way to kill us? If I'm going to be in charge, I need to know our weaknesses.'

She glanced at Jack casually, trying to gauge his

reaction. He looked thoughtful, his lips pursing, but not suspicious, she thought.

'Come on,' he said suddenly, as though he'd made up his mind. He grabbed her by the wrist and pulled, almost yanking her off her feet and through the warehouse door. She had to race after him, across the gravel parking lot and through the thin scattering of trees and waste ground beyond, and then across the highway.

'Where are we going?' Meredith gasped. Jack kept running, his hand like a vice round her wrist, tugging her onward. The sound of rushing water filled her ears, and they finally halted on a bridge, the river flowing down below.

'The others won't hear us here,' Jack told her, his voice low. 'No one else can know.' His eyes were steady on hers, searching, his hand still round her wrist. Meredith could feel her pulse pounding beneath his fingers. She nodded, her face earnest. *You can trust me.*

Whatever Jack saw in her, he seemed satisfied. 'Look,' he said, twisting sideways and bending his head so that the base of his skull was exposed to her. 'See the scar there?'

Meredith could see it, a thin white line, maybe half an inch long.

'You've got one, too,' Jack said. 'We all do. It's where the injections were administered.' He shrugged, almost bashfully. 'We're almost unkillable, but we do have an Achilles' heel. Nothing's perfect.'

'So . . .' Meredith put a hand up to feel the same place on the back of her own head.

'If we are stabbed in that exact spot, we die,' Jack said flatly. 'That's the only real danger to us I know of.'

Meredith clamped down on the hot flare of excitement rising inside her. She couldn't let Jack sense how she felt. But this was it. This was how they'd avenge Stefan, how they'd take on the latest threat. She had to let Damon know as soon as she could.

'I'll be careful,' she said.

Jack ran a cold finger down the back of her arm, and Meredith shivered. 'I know you will,' he told her, his eyes intent on hers. His fingers suddenly encircled her wrist and Meredith barely kept herself from flinching away. She needed him to trust her, to keep trusting her. Instead, she smiled, thinking of the worshipful way Sadie and the others looked at Jack, and trying to keep the same look on her own face.

'Let's go back and see how the sparring's going, shall we?' he asked. 'I don't trust Nick not to slack off if we leave them alone too long.' Meredith nodded, and they turned towards the warehouse.

But Jack hung back for a moment, his hand strong around Meredith's wrist. 'You're getting stronger and stronger,' he told her. 'If you stay loyal – if you trust me, the future will belong to us.'

Meredith nodded again stiffly, the smile fixed on her face. Jack was watching her with something close to affection in his eyes, and she felt suddenly, dizzyingly sick.

This had all gone on too long, her time here with Jack and his vampires. She was disgusted by the blood and the killing and by pretending to have turned against her husband and friends and given up on her own humanity. Now it was finally going to end. Meredith couldn't wait to betray him.

CHAPTER 17

The kid banged his fist against the bars of his cage, froth forming at the corners of his mouth, his eyes wild. His long black bangs flopped into his eyes and he shook them aside. 'You can't keep me here for ever,' he snarled, his voice low and savage. 'Locked up like this. Better to be dead.'

'Today's your lucky day, then.' Starvation didn't seem to be killing the kid, Damon thought, but he didn't look good. His already skinny face was gaunt, his cheeks hollow and his bones sharp.

The young man-made vampire swiped suddenly at Damon through the bars, hands twisted into claws, and Damon dodged out of the way. Hunger didn't seem to be making the kid any slower or weaker.

But now they knew how to kill him. Damon felt like

he was fizzing with excitement. When he looked at the kid, he didn't see just another vampire. He saw the synthetic vampires who had hunted him through Europe, who had killed Katherine. He saw Stefan's murderer.

Nothing Damon had done, none of the staking and burning and starving had helped defuse his fury.

But now, finally, he was going to get to kill him. And, after him, the rest of them. Damon realised his mouth was watering in anticipation.

He could hear the others on the basement stairs. When Meredith had called Damon to tell him about the fake vampires' vulnerable spot, he had told Elena, and of course she had called the others to join them. They'd try it out on the kid, and then they'd kill Jack.

Damon's heart filled with fierce happiness. Finally, Stefan would be avenged.

They filed in: Elena, Bonnie and Meredith, their arms linked, followed closely by Jasmine and Matt, hand in hand.

'He's looking a little skinny, Damon,' Meredith commented lightly. She was clearly buzzing with excitement, too – and why not? What she'd been working for, spying on Jack for, was finally happening.

'It doesn't matter now,' he replied, and watched the kid's eyes widen as he looked back and forth between them, picking up on something different from Damon's usual taunting. Did the young synthetic vampire know

Jack's secret? Damon thought probably not, and he shot the kid a private, vicious smile.

He turned his attention back to Meredith. 'How did you happen to discover how to kill them, anyway?' *He* knew, of course, but he wondered what Meredith had told the others.

'One of the hunters down in Atlanta accidentally hit the right spot in a fight,' she answered smoothly. 'Even Jack's luck had to run out sometime.'

'I hope it works,' Bonnie said. 'But even more, I'm just glad you're home, Meredith.' She squeezed Meredith's arm, her small face glowing with affection.

The others joined in, exclaiming about how they'd missed Meredith, and Damon took the opportunity to murmur, too low for any human to hear, 'How'd you get away?'

Meredith glanced at him over Bonnie's head with a wry smile. 'I'm supposed to be looking for you,' she murmured back. 'Killing you is pretty high on Jack's list.'

Wonderful. Damon had been hoping Jack had other things on his mind.

The young vampire was watching them, frowning in confusion. He could hear them, and he could tell Meredith was like him, of course he could. No doubt he was wondering if she'd really turned against Jack. It seemed like Jack's vampires were, on the whole, insanely loyal.

All the more reason to kill this one, so he never got a chance to report back to Jack.

'Stake,' Damon demanded, and Matt slipped one into his hand.

Before the young vampire had a chance to react, Damon had unlocked the cage and had one arm tightly around his neck, yanking his head forward to show the base of his skull. 'Scar,' Damon said, seeing the thin white line, and shoved the stake straight into it.

The point of the stake went all the way through the kid's neck, the sharp tip sticking out just below his chin in front. He gagged and choked, clawing at it, then fell to his knees, one arm still awkwardly pulled up by the handcuff connecting his wrist to the bars.

Damon stepped back and watched blood pool down the young vampire's neck and chest, puddling on the floor beneath him. The kid knocked the stake free at last, but slid limply further down the bars, supported only by the one thin arm chained to them.

He let out a harsh, blood-choked breath, and his body stiffened, his eyes rolling back into his head.

Then he lay still. He wasn't breathing. Damon listened, and heard nothing: no heartbeat, no struggle to breathe.

'We did it,' Meredith said softly. Her eyes were wide and shining with excitement.

'Wow,' Matt said. 'That was, um . . . surprisingly easy.'

With a sudden jerk, the vampire spasmed on the floor, his eyes flying open. Then he leapt to his feet, his handcuff rattling. The gash in his neck was healing, new pink skin stretching across it. He growled and swiped at Damon through the bars. Damon, caught off balance, stumbled and almost fell. The vampire's sharp nails cut into his leg, and Damon shook him off, swearing.

It didn't work. Damon could feel Elena's leaden misery filling him, mixing with his own red-hot rage.

'I'm sorry,' he said, desperately, and reached for her hand.

Then the back of his neck began to prickle uncomfortably. Something wrong, getting closer.

Jack's voice, as cold as ice, came suddenly from behind them. 'Meredith, I expected so much more from you.'

Damon whipped around.

Jack was at the end of the row of dusty cages, flanked by a crowd of his vampires. A long hunting knife gleamed in his hand.

'It was a trap,' Meredith said flatly.

'Of course it was a trap,' Jack said, his lips curling into a sneer. 'It was a test, too, and you failed.'

With that, Jack and his vampires charged.

Two of them, a stocky guy and a blonde-haired girl, slammed into Damon, one on each side, the girl driving her arm against his throat while the guy swept a leg against Damon's, trying to knock him off balance.

The move felt like one of Meredith's to him. She'd been teaching them. *Wonderful*, he thought, grabbing the guy's leg and flinging him backward on to the hard concrete floor. The last thing they needed was a crowd of vampire hunter-trained vampires. He managed to snap the girl's neck, giving himself some breathing room, but he knew she wouldn't stay down for long.

Snarling, Damon looked around for Elena and saw that she was safe for the moment. She was in a corner at one end of the long row of storage cages, her hands extended. The air shimmered slightly around her. She must be making some sort of Guardian force field around herself, because no vampire was coming near her. As he watched, the shimmer around her expanded, encompassing the rest of their group for a moment, but then it shrank back. She was trying to protect them all, but it didn't look like she could work up the Power.

Matt had Jasmine and Bonnie backed into a corner behind him and was swinging a stave at the lanky vampire coming towards them, driving it into him again and again. The vampire flinched under the blows, but kept coming forward, his wounds healing faster than Matt could inflict them.

Bonnie was fumbling in her purse, no doubt looking for a weapon. Matt was no coward, but the vampire was just toying with him – one quick move, and the human would fall. Before Damon could spring forward to save the girls, Meredith was there, slamming the other vampire against the wall and efficiently breaking his neck.

There was the rattle of metal behind him, and suddenly someone landed on Damon's back, thin strong arms twining around his throat. He automatically slammed his back against the wall, forcing a grunt of pain from his assailant. A sharp edge of metal – handcuffs, Damon realised – on his opponent's wrist pressed against Damon's throat. Someone had let the kid loose from his cage.

The young vampire was furious and half mad with hunger. He clung on tight and bit down, working his sharp fangs savagely into Damon's neck.

Damon slammed backward into the wall again, trying to get rid of him. The kid's desperation gave him strength, though, and he held on tighter.

Distracted by the young vampire, Damon almost missed Bonnie's fierce gesture, her hands shooting up into the air. There was a burst of blinding white light and suddenly Damon was flying backward.

His elbow scraped painfully along the floor as the force of Bonnie's explosion shoved him along, but at least it had knocked the kid off his back. They landed side by side, and glared at each other, both flat on the ground and gasping with effort. The kid's mouth was sloppy with blood.

All the vampires were on the ground, Damon

realised. Jack was the fastest back on his feet, and he dragged Meredith up with him, his long knife pressed tightly against her throat. A thin line of blood dripped down Meredith's neck, soaking the edge of her dark-blue T-shirt.

Everyone froze. Damon could hear the young vampire panting beside him, but he couldn't tear his eyes off Meredith, not even to snap the kid's neck.

'Go ahead,' Meredith said bitterly. 'Cut my head off. See if that'll kill me.'

Jack smiled. 'Oh, I know how to kill you,' he said softly. 'But that would be giving you what you want.' His eyes flicked to Damon. 'Immortality's quite the curse, isn't it, Salvatore?'

Faster than even Damon's eyes could follow, Jack stabbed the knife viciously down, cutting through Meredith's stomach. Then he let go and let her fall. Meredith dropped to her knees, her hands desperately trying to hold the gaping wound together. Bonnie screamed, and Matt shouted, 'Meredith!' sounding horrified. Damon only winced – that looked painful.

As they watched, the wound began to heal. In just a few seconds, Meredith's flesh was whole again beneath the rip in her shirt. Elena gasped, and Jasmine whimpered.

Jack's smile spread wider. 'I thought you must have been lying to them. What do you think they'll say, now that they know you're one of mine?'

Bonnie began to chant in Latin, her voice hard and furious. A moment later, Elena joined her. She raised her hands above her head, seeming to draw on their energy, and a shimmer appeared above her.

Jack eyed them, and then grinned at Damon. 'I'll see you soon, Salvatore.' He snapped his fingers, and in a moment his vampires were with him.

Damon pulled himself to his feet, ready to continue the fight, but Jack and his team were already gone. Damon could hear their footfalls, faint and far away.

Meredith, her face ghost-pale, climbed slowly to her feet. Her wound was already closing. She looked at her friends, who were staring back at her. Eyes wet, she looked from one human to another, taking in their horror. Damon could hear her heart pounding and her shaky, panicked breaths.

'I – I . . .' Meredith grasped the edges of her cut shirt and pulled them together, as if to hide the evidence of what she was. But she'd been revealed. There was no way to hide it now.

CHAPTER
18

'**Y**ou knew about Meredith, didn't you?' Elena asked Damon. After the first shock of discovery wore off, she had tried to get Meredith to come home with them. Her friend had seemed so lost. But Meredith had slid away, saying she had to go home and talk to Alaric. She hadn't held eye contact with Elena, either, her eyes flitting down, her face averted. Meredith was ashamed, Elena realised.

Now Elena and Damon were alone in Elena's apartment, side by side on the couch. She felt exhausted; she just wanted to lay her head on Damon's shoulder and close her eyes.

Damon looked at Elena, assessing, and then nodded warily. 'She didn't want me to tell anyone.'

Elena paused. 'Thank you,' she said sincerely.

Damon arched an eyebrow curiously. Clearly, thanks hadn't been what he was expecting.

'Remember when I became a vampire?' Elena asked.

'Believe me, princess, that's not something I would forget.'

'Me neither.' Elena shivered. It had been a bad time for her. Fell's Church was falling apart around them and everyone had thought – had needed to think – that Elena was dead. She had been lonely and frightened and almost out of her mind at the changes she was experiencing. 'You took care of me,' she told Damon. 'Without you, I wouldn't have survived. I'm glad Meredith had you to turn to.'

Damon tilted his head, staring at her, his midnight-black eyes unreadable. 'I know you want to think I'm a good person, Elena,' he said slowly. 'But I didn't help Meredith through the change, and I didn't protect her. She wouldn't have thanked me if I had.'

Without really meaning to, Elena leaned closer to Damon. 'You would have helped her if she'd wanted you to,' she said, sure that this was true.

The corner of Damon's mouth turned up in a half-smile. 'For your sake, Elena,' he said softly. 'Anything I do for any of them, for anyone, it's for you. Always. You know that.'

She did know that. Deep inside, Elena was certain that she was the only one who connected Damon to anyone else, now that Stefan was gone.

The bond between them throbbed, sweet, sharp emotion spilling through it, and Damon leaned even closer to her. His lips were only millimetres away from hers. She could feel his cool breath. He moved closer still, his perfect lips parting.

Elena almost leaned in and took what Damon was offering. She wanted him, she did, and she could feel the love he would give her. But there was something cold and hard inside her, like a ball of ice in the centre of her chest. If she did this, it would be moving on. It would be letting go of Stefan.

Elena pulled back. 'I can't,' she said. 'I'm sorry. Stefan . . .'

With one swift, smooth movement, Damon was standing, turned away from her so that she couldn't see his face. 'Of course,' he said quietly. 'He'll always be between us, won't he? Even if we live for ever.'

Through their bond, Elena felt a sharp stinging pain. It brought tears to her eyes, but it only lasted for a few seconds before Damon muffled it, blocking the link between them to no more than a buzz. He still wouldn't look at her.

Suddenly chilled, Elena folded her arms around herself. It was possible that they would live for ever, wasn't it? Un-ageing, unchanging, for ever young. Without Stefan.

'I'm sorry,' she said again. Damon nodded once, stiffly, and walked away, across the living room and through the door to the kitchen. A moment later, she heard the apartment door close quietly behind him.

What did I do? She pressed her hands against her chest, feeling a hollow, desperate ache inside. She couldn't tell if the emotion belonged to her or to Damon.

Evening had come while Meredith sat on her and Alaric's bed, waiting for Alaric to come home from teaching his class at Dalcrest. Dread pooled inside her. Half of her – more than half of her – just wanted to run, to get away before she saw him. She closed her eyes and clenched her fists so tight that her nails bit into her palms.

She had been waiting for hours. By the time she heard the front door open and close, the bedroom was almost totally dark, lit only by the streetlights shining in from outside.

Of course, Meredith could see perfectly well.

'Alaric,' she said in a small voice, unsure if he could hear her from the hall. He called back and then came to the bedroom.

'Hey,' he said softly. 'When did you get home?' Even if she hadn't been able to see the smile on his face, she would have heard it in his voice. 'How come it's so dark in here?' He reached towards the light switch, and Meredith stiffened.

'Leave it off, OK?'

'What's wrong?' Alaric came closer and brushed a

concerned hand featherlight across her cheek. Meredith pulled him down beside her on the bed and buried her head in his shoulder. She could hear his heart beating, as steady as the sea.

'What is it?' Alaric asked, pulling her against him. His body was warm and solid, and he petted her hair with one hand, trying to calm her down. Meredith realised she was shaking against Alaric, pushing her face against his shoulder. 'Sweetheart, what's wrong?' he asked again, sounding almost frantic now.

Meredith told him everything she could think of: how Jack had changed her, how long she'd been hiding it from him. That she'd lied, that she hadn't been down in Atlanta with the hunters at all, but with Jack, being a vampire.

'I couldn't stay here. I couldn't trust myself.' *Around you*, she didn't add.

Alaric was silent for a moment, and tears began to fall from Meredith's eyes. She pressed her face against his shoulder again, shaking. His shirt was warm with his body heat, and she pushed closer, treasuring the last moments of contact. He'd leave her. He'd have to. How could Alaric love her, if she was a monster?

But then his arms went around her and held her tightly.

'We'll get through this,' he promised. His lips brushed the side of her head, and she gave a choked sob, soaking Alaric's shoulder with tears and snot. 'There'll be a cure. Maybe. And even if not, we love each other. We can handle this.'

Alaric's voice was strained, but he wasn't flinching away from her. And there weren't any lies between them, not now. She closed her eyes and sobbed into his shoulder.

She could still smell his blood, salty and metallic, as rich and mysterious as the ocean. But Alaric didn't smell like food any more. Instead, he smelled like home.

CHAPTER

19

Matt hesitated in the hallway, Jasmine's hand firmly in his, staring at the plain wooden door to Meredith and Alaric's apartment. His mouth felt dry, and he wasn't breathing quite right.

It was ridiculous, he knew. He wasn't afraid of Meredith just because she was suddenly a vampire. He'd been friends with Stefan for years, and he had a cordial relationship with Damon, although they weren't exactly friends. He'd even been in love with a vampire, poor Chloe, when he was a freshman in college.

Maybe his history with Chloe was the trouble. He knew how hard it was for a vampire to resist feeding, to stay a person instead of a killer. Chloe hadn't been able to, and in the end she'd chosen to die instead. Becoming a vampire, fighting against those new, violent instincts, could tear a good person apart.

Matt wasn't going to let that happen to Meredith. None of them were.

Jasmine leaned against him, warm and quietly reassuring. 'Can't stand out here all day,' she said, and Matt lifted his hand and knocked.

Alaric opened the door and smiled at them, looking so normal that Matt's heart gave a ridiculous hopeful hop. *Maybe everything's OK.*

But, as the door swung wider, he saw Meredith, slumped at the kitchen table, her head in her hands, and his heart sank again. Meredith was definitely not OK. She looked broken. Like she'd been fighting on, out of pride, pretending everything was fine, fiercely determined that none of them would know what had happened to her. And now that they knew, all that fight had gone.

Damon lounged in a chair on the other side of the table from Meredith, while Elena and Bonnie leaned against the counter behind him, their faces troubled. Out of the corner of his eye, Matt registered Zander coming in from the other room, moving with an easy, animal grace. But Matt's attention was fixed on Meredith. He couldn't believe she was a vampire. And they hadn't known.

'I can hear your heart thumping, Matt,' Meredith said, not raising her head. 'You're scared of me.'

It was the flat bitterness in her tone that got Matt

moving towards her; she was one of his dearest friends, he couldn't let her sound like that, feel that way. She looked up at him, her grey eyes wide and wet, and warmth flooded him.

'I'm not scared,' he said, reaching out for her. She flinched away for a second and then leaned into his hand, her body as warm and solid as it had always been. 'Meredith, it doesn't matter.' She gave a tear-choked snort at that, and he reconsidered, squeezing her shoulders. 'OK, of course it matters, but you haven't changed. You're still the same girl who shared your lunch with me in kindergarten.'

He could remember her so clearly at age five, tall and solemn, dark hair pulled into pigtails. On their first day, Matt had forgotten the lunch his mom had carefully packed for him, and burst into tears in the cafeteria. Meredith had been there, calm and compassionate, giving him half of her peanut butter sandwich, a handful of grapes, breaking her cookie neatly in two. Matt had tagged along after her for the rest of that whole long confusing first day, confident that Meredith would look after him.

'I trust you, Mer,' he went on. 'Jack did something terrible to you – really awful, and God, I'm so sorry about that. But I'm not scared. Because I know that you're still the girl who was the only person I could talk to when Elena went to France that summer in high school and I worried she was going to break up with me. You're still the same girl who was the total champion of our fifth-grade soccer team.' His eyes were stinging, and he swiped a hand across them. 'I know that girl, Meredith, and I know she's good all the way through. I'd never be scared of you.'

Meredith gave a choked-off laugh and bit her lip. 'I know – I know all those things about the past, Matt. But what if I can't help myself? I hear your blood pumping through your veins, louder than the words you're saying. You smell like food.'

'They've always smelled like dinner to me, but I manage to restrain myself,' Damon told her, with a narrow smile. 'Mostly. And you're much more moral than I am, hunter.'

'One more thing I know about you is that you're too tough to give in to anything like that,' Matt said. 'I've got faith in you. We all do.'

'And we are going to help you,' Bonnie said, folding her arms. Her small chin was stuck out stubbornly. 'Alaric and I are going to figure out a cure.'

Damon was the one who laughed that time. 'The only cure for being a vampire is a sharp stake, little redbird,' he said gently.

'With my magic and Alaric's research skills . . .' Bonnie's shoulders rose in a tiny, hopeful shrug. 'Maybe? Maybe we can do this?'

'I'll help,' Jasmine said quickly. 'He used science to make his vampires. Maybe science can cure them.'

Meredith's eyes were brighter now, not quite so defeated, and Matt fumbled in his pocket. 'I brought you something,' he told her, his fingers fastening around a thin chain as he pulled it out of his pocket. It was a cheap silver-toned bracelet with a heart frame charm.

'Is that from prom?' Elena asked, surprised.

The bracelets had been favours at their junior prom. Matt and Elena had gone together, and each seat at the table – which they'd shared with Bonnie and Meredith and their dates – had one in front of it, the frame ready to hold a tiny copy of the owner's prom picture. Matt had kept his; he was the sentimental type. And he'd dug it up last night and scraped out the photo of his and Elena's smiling faces, back before everything began. He spent some time in Photoshop, shrinking down another old picture to fit.

'It's us,' Meredith said softly, looking down at the tiny picture. It was from the first day of college: Matt, Meredith, Bonnie and Elena smiling up from the heart-shaped frame, arms around each other's necks. And Stefan beside Elena, with them but somehow separate, his classically handsome face solemn. Meredith touched his face lightly with one finger, and Matt sighed. He missed Stefan. They all did.

'I thought if you had it, it would remind you of how much we love you. You're one of us, whether you're a vampire or a human. We'll be here to help you remember who you are.' Matt licked his lips nervously.

'We believe in you.' Elena leaned forward to wrap an arm around Meredith's shoulder. 'And we love you.'

Bonnie nodded, reaching to pat Meredith's back.

Meredith's lips tightened as if she was trying not to cry, and then she blinked and looked up at Matt. 'Thank you,' she said simply, and wrapped the bracelet around her wrist.

'Let me,' Alaric said, bending to work the catch.

'Touching,' Damon said dryly. 'We all know the hunter's as tough as nails; she'll be all right.' His voice was flat, but his eyes lingered on Meredith with something that, to Matt's surprise, looked almost like sympathy. 'The important thing now is, what are we going to do about her maker? We know where Jack's headquarters are, but we've got no idea how to kill him. And now he's on to Meredith, so she can't spy on him any more.'

'Sorry,' Meredith said.

Damon's shoulders rose in a languid shrug. 'You tried. But what's the next step?'

'The next step is me,' Elena said decisively. Her dark-blue eyes were shining. 'If we can't beat Jack by fighting him, we have to figure out his weakness. Since infiltrating his camp didn't work out, we have to find Siobhan.'

'But you've looked for her,' Bonnie objected.

Elena shook her head. 'Not hard enough. I've been

trying to pick up traces of her aura, and I'm beginning to think she's left town. If Damon and I drive around the area, maybe I'll be able to find something to lead us in the right direction.' She looked towards Zander, who had been hanging back, watching them all quietly. 'While we're doing that, can the Pack patrol Dalcrest and look out for vampires? Protect everybody?'

Zander nodded. 'We'll do what we can.'

Inwardly, Matt sighed a little. The Pack would patrol. Elena and Damon would hunt for Siobhan. Alaric, Bonnie and Jasmine would search for a cure for Meredith's vampirism. It would have been nice if Matt, for once, was able to really help.

But then Meredith looked up at him and smiled – a tiny, crooked smile, but a real one. 'Thank you, Matt,' she said again, running her fingers over the bracelet. A spark flared in Matt's chest. Maybe this time, it would all be OK in the end. Maybe.

Elena waited for everyone else to leave. When the others had gone, Damon pushed himself away from the table and looked at Elena expectantly. 'Shall we hit the road?' he asked. 'Start the hunt for Siobhan?'

'You go on without me,' she said. 'I'll meet you back at home and we can get started.' He nodded once and strode off without looking back, as sleek and graceful as a panther.

Still Elena lingered, standing uncertainly by the

counter as Alaric began to collect glasses and take them to the sink.

'What's up?' Meredith asked finally, tipping her head back from where she was sitting to look up at Elena, her long dark hair spilling across her shoulders. 'You're hovering.'

'Walk me to the door,' Elena said quietly. She didn't want Alaric to overhear what she was going to say. Let it be Meredith's choice first.

Meredith arched one elegant eyebrow curiously and, for a moment, looked just like her old self. She got up and followed Elena.

Elena remembered her transition as a vampire. All the sensations tugging at you, the ever-present hunger. But it must be harder for Meredith, because being a vampire, the one thing she'd been raised to hunt and kill, would be the worst thing Meredith could imagine. The look of devastation on Meredith's face, the way she pulled in on herself as if expecting a blow, hurt Elena to see.

And yet . . .

It wasn't all bad, was it? Elena didn't like to think about the fact that, except for Damon, her friends were getting older and she . . . wasn't. They would become middle-aged, maybe have kids, get old. They would die.

But not Elena. And not Meredith. Not any more. Wasn't that something to be thankful for?

'Here,' Elena said softly. She felt in her purse and

drew out a half-full water bottle. It felt the same as any other bottle of water in her hand, but the liquid inside shimmered, a tiny touch of gold to it. Meredith's eyes widened.

'Is that . . . ?' she asked hesitantly, and Elena nodded.

'It's from the Fountain of Eternal Life and Youth,' she said. 'I thought . . .' She felt weirdly uncomfortable. 'For Alaric. Just in case. It's hard, when one of you ages and the other doesn't. I know, for me and Stefan . . .'

Elena hesitated again. It had been the right choice for her at the time. She hadn't wanted to grow old while Stefan, by her side, stayed young and healthy, year after year.

When she had drunk the water, in a room filled with candlelight and sweet-smelling flowers, she had been filled with joy. She had chosen Stefan, and that was the moment of her promise – more than that, her sacred vow: They would be together, for eternity.

But now she was alone. For ever.

Elena's breath hitched. She shook off the feeling. It wouldn't be like that for Meredith and Alaric.

But Meredith stepped back, tucking her hands behind her back as if she was afraid to touch the bottle. Her lips were parting to speak, but then Alaric came down the hall. Elena could see from his face that he had overheard, after all.

'Thank you,' he said, and took the bottle from Elena's hand. 'Just in case.'

Elena hugged them both briefly and left them alone. She hoped she'd made the right decision. But Elena couldn't make the choice for them.

It wasn't the same, Elena knew that now. Not ageing, not changing. The idea of living for ever without Stefan hurt her, a deep sore ache that never left her for a moment. If she'd known that she'd be without him, she wouldn't have drunk the waters. She would have chosen to live a normal life, to grow old, to grow up, to die.

But things would be different for Meredith and Alaric. And if Elena and Damon could find out Siobhan's secrets, if they could somehow find a cure for this artificial vampirism that infected Meredith, they would never have to make that choice. Meredith and Alaric would both be human again and could grow old together. She knew that was what Meredith would choose, if she had the chance.

Elena straightened her shoulders and walked more swiftly down the hall, the heels of her boots clicking determinedly. She didn't want to leave Meredith's side, not when she was suffering. But if Elena's mission was successful, then perhaps Meredith's suffering could end.

CHAPTER

20

The street lamps threw pools of light on to the dark sidewalk, and Bonnie and Zander walked from shadow to light to shadow, hand in hand. The day had been hot, but in the fifteen minutes or so since they'd left Meredith and Alaric's apartment, it had gotten chilly. It felt like it was going to rain, and Bonnie shivered.

She snuck a peek at Zander out of the corner of her eye as they went, but his face was shadowed, the lights shining off his white-blond hair, and she couldn't read him.

'Poor Meredith,' she said hesitantly. Why did she feel so awkward talking to him suddenly? This was Zander.

'Mmm-hmm,' Zander said, not looking at her. He was gazing straight ahead, intently, a tiny crease between his eyebrows, as if he was thinking hard.

He'd barely said anything at Meredith's, hanging back when he should have been participating, helping. She opened her mouth to say something – anything – and closed it again. She squeezed his hand instead, but he didn't seem to notice.

They turned and began to walk past the botanical gardens towards home. A breeze blew Bonnie's hair across her face and the warm smell of summer roses came through the fence, a heavy, seductive scent. It could have been such a romantic moment that tears rose in Bonnie's eyes. On a night like this, everything should be perfect.

Bonnie stopped dead under a streetlight.

'What is it?' asked Zander, coming to a halt beside her.

'"What is it?"' Bonnie mimicked. She was furious suddenly, adrenalin pumping through her. 'You've been acting like a total weirdo for days! And now you're not even talking to me?'

Zander blinked. 'What?' His face was washed out by the pale light, his gorgeous blue eyes looking grey.

'Don't you 'what' me!' Bonnie snapped. 'God, Zander, I thought you were braver than just blowing me off. If you want to break up with me, just do it.' Hot tears were beginning to stream down her cheeks and she could feel her nose starting to run. She was an ugly, messy crier, and she hated it. 'You're being a jerk,' she said thickly, letting go of Zander's hand to wipe her eyes with her arm.

'Bonnie – no,' Zander sounded desperate. 'I don't want to break up with you. I – this isn't the way I planned it.' He took her hand again, tightly, and pulled her further down the sidewalk, then through the gate to the botanical garden.

The scent of the roses was even stronger here, almost dizzying. Leaves brushed against Bonnie's arms as Zander led her to a bench beneath an arch of climbing white roses.

'What's going on?' Bonnie asked, sitting down, wiping at her eyes again. Fallen rose petals dotted the bench, and she flicked some of them off. A soft rumble of thunder came from far away.

Zander dropped to his knees in the dirt at her feet. 'I don't want to break up with you, Bonnie. I want to marry you.'

All the air rushed out of Bonnie's chest. She opened her mouth to say something, but all she could do was squeak. *Yes. Yes.*

She reached forward and pulled him towards her. Zander shuffled closer, still on his knees. Their lips met, and a warm thrill shot through her. *Here you are.* This was the Zander she'd been looking for, his lips quirking into a smile and his eyes wide and loving and fixed on her, seeing her again.

'Wait,' he said, breaking the kiss. 'I've got – I've been

carrying it around, waiting for the right time.' He dug in his pocket and pulled out a small velvet box.

It was a ring. An amazingly gorgeous ring, shiny and bright, one big round-cut glittering stone on a golden band. 'Will you?' Zander asked, holding it out.

'OK,' Bonnie said. She was still breathless, but she could speak now, and she was absolutely sure. She was smiling so hard her cheeks hurt. There was nothing she wanted more than to marry Zander. 'OK. I'd love to marry you.'

She was purely, blindingly happy. And behind that white glow of joy was a contented planning hum: *have to call my mom, bridesmaids – Elena and Meredith and my sisters all look good in blue, big fluffy white dress.*

But Zander didn't slide the ring on to her finger. He stayed on his knees looking up at her. 'I need to tell you something first.' He licked his lips nervously and reached out to take her hand again. 'The Pack has to leave Dalcrest. I want you to come with us.'

Bonnie felt her mouth drop into an O of surprise. 'What? Come where?'

Running his free hand through his hair, Zander sighed and sat back on his heels. 'I've tried to find a way out of it. I didn't want to have to tell you unless it was definite. I appealed to the High Wolf Council, but they said we'd been here a lot longer than they'd originally planned. They've cut me a lot of slack because I'm the Alpha and I wanted to stay, but now they say there's trouble in Colourado and they want us there.'

'There's trouble here!' Bonnie said indignantly.

'I know. But it's Pack stuff. In the end, I'm sworn to them and I have to do what they say. The whole Pack has to go where we're needed.' He squeezed her hand tightly and looked back up at her, his eyes pleading. 'Come with us. Marry me. I don't want to lose you, Bonnie.'

Bonnie couldn't breathe. And it wasn't with the happy surprise of a few moments ago. Instead her throat seemed to be closing up. She felt like she was going to die.

Colourado. Colourado was really far away.

The first tiny drops of rain hit her arms, one cold drop and then another. Wind blew through the rose arch and showered damp white petals down over Bonnie. One hit her face, a delicate blow, and she peeled it off her own cheek, soft and wilted.

It was beginning to rain more steadily, and the cold raindrops loosened Bonnie's tongue and let her start thinking again. 'I can't. Zander, I can't.' He was staring at her, his eyelashes wet with rain. 'I love you, but how could I leave here with everything that's going on? Meredith's a vampire. Stefan's dead. My friends need me here.'

Zander leaned closer, put a hand on Bonnie's knee to steady himself. 'I need you,' he said softly, almost whispering.

Rain plastered Bonnie's hair against her forehead and ran down her cheeks, feeling almost like tears. 'Please, Zander, I can't.'

Zander's eyes closed for a second, long pale eyelashes fanning against his cheeks, and then he opened his eyes, let go of her hand, and stood. 'I understand,' he said, his voice flat. 'I'll go tomorrow, OK? I don't want to make things tense for everybody. Some of the guys can stay and patrol for a few days, until Damon and Elena are back.' Standing above her, he seemed impossibly tall. Bonnie couldn't get a good look at his face, but his hands were clenched tightly. He backed away from her for a few steps, then turned and headed for the gate out of the botanical gardens, walking slowly with his head down.

Water was running down her arms, soaking her clothes. A white rose petal clung limply to the back of her hand, and Bonnie stared at it numbly, seeing the curve at its base, the line of brown at its edge. There was a terrible ache in her chest. Bonnie realised she was feeling her heart break.

CHAPTER

21

It had rained all night and through the day, and now it was late afternoon, the cloudy grey sky gradually getting darker. Damon drove his gleaming black car down the highway and let his Power loose around him, trying to sense if anything supernatural lurked in the woods on either side of the road. There was nothing, just the gentle hum of nondescript human minds from the cars on the road and the towns they swept by.

'There's just a trace,' Elena said from the passenger seat beside him. She leaned forward and peered out through the windshield. 'It's very faint, but I think she kept heading north.'

They'd been on the road all day. Elena swore they were following slight signs of Siobhan's aura. Damon couldn't see them himself, but he trusted her. She'd always been clever. Terribly, frighteningly young, but clever. And he could feel her intentness coming through the bond between them, the careful way she scanned their environment, her excitement when she caught a glimpse of Siobhan's aura trail. Sitting so close to her, he was more aware of her emotions than ever.

And now he was feeling something else from her. Hunger. He was about to comment, when she stretched, and said, 'Let's get something to eat.'

Damon felt his mouth twitch up into the beginnings of a smile – he'd read her so well – and he took the next exit. He drove a little further, until they came to a likely-looking diner. They pulled into the parking lot and climbed out, glancing up at the sullen glow of the low-hanging sun through the clouds. It would be evening soon, and it didn't feel like they were getting much closer to their goal.

Crossing to the other side of the car, he opened Elena's door for her. 'Come on, princess,' he said. 'The quest will wait while you have a cheeseburger.'

Inside the diner, gingham tablecloths covered each table, folk art pictures of roosters and ducks hung on the walls, and a child's toy – an Etch-a-Sketch, Magic 8 Ball or game – sat on each table.

'Aw, this is charming,' Elena said as the waitress, wearing a ruffled apron, led them to a table for two.

'The word you're looking for is cloying,' Damon told

her. The waitress glanced back at him and he shot her a blinding smile.

Elena ordered a sandwich and iced tea, but Damon didn't feel like eating. Human food gave him no nourishment, and there was nothing on the menu he was in the mood to sample. There was a low ache of hunger in his stomach, though, and he ran his tongue over his sensitive canines. He could last a little longer before he hunted, he supposed. He wasn't desperate enough yet for fur or feathers in his mouth. 'Just coffee, please,' he told the waitress.

'Want to play checkers while we wait?' Elena asked, stacking the red and black pieces across the miniature game board sitting on their table.

'Checkers?' Damon said with slight distaste.

'Sure, it'll be fun.' Elena said. Damon hesitated for a split second, and Elena's eyes widened. 'You don't know how to play checkers?'

'You'd be amazed how often it doesn't come up,' Damon said dryly.

'Still,' Elena said. 'You're more than five hundred years old. You never learned? Five-year-olds can play checkers.'

'They didn't when I was five,' Damon snapped. He felt ridiculously embarrassed – it wasn't like he wanted to play a child's game. 'I can play chess.'

'I suppose that is much more suave and creature-of-the-night,' Elena agreed thoughtfully. 'Come on, let me show you. Checkers is easy.'

There was a teasing glow in her eyes, and Damon couldn't resist her. The checkers clicked together as she stacked them, and he took a moment to bask in the warmth coming through the bond between them. She still loved Stefan, he knew it, but she cared for Damon, too. 'Go ahead,' he told her. 'Whatever you want.'

Elena shot him a quick, triumphant grin. 'OK,' she said brightly, laying the checkers out on the board between them, black ones in front of Damon, red ones in front of herself. 'So, you move diagonally forward, only on the dark squares. And if you're next to one of my pieces and there's an empty space on the other side, you can jump over it, and capture it. When you get to my side of the board, your piece gets kinged and can move forward and backward. You win if you get all my pieces off the board.'

'I see.' Damon sat back and regarded the board thoughtfully, pushing back the little swell of glee inside him so that Elena wouldn't feel it through their bond. This game was just Alquerque, which had already been old when he was a child, only played on a chessboard. 'I think I can handle it.'

Elena went first, and Damon bided his time for several moves. Then she jumped two of his pieces, sitting back with a smirk. 'And that's how you do it,' she said, pleased with herself.

'Impressive,' Damon said coolly, eyeing a hole she'd

left in her defenCes. Instead of taking advantage, he ignored the opening and moved another piece forward.

It was good to see Elena enjoying herself for a moment. She'd been too sad for too long. *Maybe*, Damon thought. *Maybe someday she'll get over Stefan*. It was a betrayal of his little brother, but he couldn't help the flush of hope the thought gave him. After all, Damon had all the time in the world to wait.

'You'll get it,' Elena said encouragingly, taking another one of his pieces. 'Checkers isn't hard, I promise.' There was a smug little curl at the edge of her lips.

'Indeed,' Damon said. He could hear the waitress at the counter behind him, smell the warm salt of Elena's fries. Lunch was ready. He leaned forward and jumped four of her men with a satisfying series of clicks. 'King me.'

Elena blinked at the board, and Damon let a smile spread over his face. 'You must be a wonderful teacher,' he told her.

Elena's cheeks were prettily flushed, and she glanced up at him through her lashes as they crossed the parking lot together. Her arm pressed against his, and Damon was gloriously aware of the heat coming off her silky skin.

'You're a quick learner,' she commented. 'I can't believe you won every game.'

Damon vaguely noted a few figures at the edge of the parking lot, looking towards them, and checked absently – human, harmless – his attention fixed on Elena. He watched as they got into their car and drove away. He'd been right: human.

'My life's been long enough – ' he began, and then a heavy body slammed into him, low and hard, knocking the breath out of him.

Vampires.

Damon hit the ground and rolled, grappling with the synthetic vampire above him. His back scraped painfully against the asphalt of the parking lot. A heavy, dark-skinned, muscular man, older than most of Jack's protégés, snarled down at him, his teeth sharp and glaringly white against his skin.

'Damon!' Elena shouted.

The vampire pressed forward, his teeth scraping at Damon's throat, and Damon yanked away. The vampire's body was warm, as warm as a human's, and his breath was hot and fetid, like something rotten. Damon shoved at him, trying to get some leverage to snap his neck. But his weight was too much – his canines sank into Damon's throat, tearing at it.

The bite burned like fire, and Damon thrashed, trying to get free.

Out of the corner of his eye, he caught more movement. Another vampire. Two vampires. No.

With a fresh surge of strength, Damon struggled

harder, rolling over and slamming the larger vampire down against the asphalt of the parking lot. He needed to get up before the other two got to Elena. Maybe they couldn't kill her, not with their bite, but they could take her, and Jack knew Elena's secret. It was unlikely that she'd be able to raise her Guardian Powers against them – they weren't her target, and she had no time to coax her Power to the surface.

He and the artificial vampire were gripping each other tight now, straining against each other. The other vampire's muscles bulged with effort. Slowly, his teeth gritted, Damon forced his opponent's arms back down and pinned them against the pavement, enjoying the expression of shock on his face.

He snapped the other vampire's neck quickly and watched as his eyes glazed over. That would keep him down for a little while. Damon leapt gracefully to his feet.

As he turned, he heard a heavy thump. Behind him, a tall light-haired vampire had fallen at Elena's feet, a stake protruding from his chest. The third vampire, a woman, hesitated, staring at Elena.

Before the fallen recovered, Damon took two long steps over and snapped her neck quickly. 'That'll knock her out longer than the stake,' he told Elena, and bent to snap the neck of the third vampire as well.

'We'd better get out of here while we can,' Elena said. She bent to tug her stake, with an audible huff of effort, from the tall vampire's chest. Efficiently, she wiped it on a tissue and tucked the stake back into her purse.

'Nicely done,' Damon said, trying to gauge her mood. She didn't seem frightened, and there was nothing but adrenalin-fuelled excitement and a certain smug pleasure coming through their bond. 'You don't need too much protecting, do you, Guardian?' Elena smirked at him, and he felt her spark of pride.

Then her face fell. The pride shifted to shock, then fear. 'You're hurt,' she said.

'Oh,' Damon said, reaching up to touch the bite. The blood was still trickling down his neck, hot and painful. He'd forgotten for a moment in his concern for Elena. 'I'm all right.'

'No,' Elena said. 'Come here.' She leaned back against the side of the car and pulled open the neck of her shirt, brushing back her hair from her throat. She cocked her head invitingly.

He could see the delicate veins beneath her skin, and his breath caught. Elena would be so soft, he knew, her neck like warm satin beneath his lips and teeth. And her blood was rich and sweet.

'Hurry,' she said urgently. 'They'll be waking up soon.'

Damon wanted. He really did.

But he swallowed and dragged his eyes away from her, licking his lips.

When he'd fed from her before, she'd turned away from him. She hadn't wanted him to see inside her mind, hadn't wanted him any closer than the bond between them already brought them.

He didn't just want her blood. When he drank from Elena, he didn't want it to be about food.

'No thank you, princess,' he said. 'I'm fine.'

'Don't be chivalrous, Damon,' Elena said, irritated. 'You need this.'

Damon stared down at his feet. 'Better not,' he said. 'We need to get going.' He took a quick breath, and then looked up at Elena again, shooting her his most brilliant smile. 'I really am perfectly fine. It's healing already.' He brought his hand up to his neck, and found that it was true: The bite was messy and painful, but the wound was clotting.

Before she could argue, he opened his car door and reached over to unlock hers. Once they were in, he pulled out, tyres squealing. The false vampires were already beginning to stir.

Elena felt a bit petulant, he thought, cautiously checking their bond – his princess liked everyone to fall in line with her plans – and he concentrated on shutting down the connection between them, trying to broadcast only thoughts about the road ahead.

He didn't know if she could feel the small bitter ache in his chest, but he surrounded it with layers of *don't ask* and *private* and hoped she would mind her own business.

'You're being an idiot,' Elena told him sharply. Damon winced, and didn't answer. The warmth that had echoed through their bond earlier was gone.

He couldn't bear to drink from her any more.

It was an exquisite torture, tasting her sweetness, reaching out for her mind, her soul – only to have Elena pull away. Sharing blood like that should be for lovers, the most intimate connection there was.

Damon was tired of letting himself pretend. Stefan – his irritating, noble, beloved little brother – was dead, but he still occupied Elena's heart. And if Damon couldn't have that place, if that part of Elena was going to be closed to him, he had to let it go.

CHAPTER

22

'Let's get just one more vial,' Jasmine coaxed, and Meredith held out her arm.

'Don't you think you've taken enough blood today?' Matt asked, his forehead crinkling with concern. 'You're turning her into a pincushion.'

'It's fine,' Meredith said tiredly. She hadn't fed properly for days – just the occasional bird or beast – and her jaw ached. She felt slightly sick, and the smell of the blood flowing beneath Matt and Jasmine's skin made her light-headed. She blinked and tried to focus on what they were saying, which had been much easier when she was with Jack and the others. The regular human blood diet had kept her sharp.

Maybe Jasmine could hook her up with blood from the hospital.

Tightening her lips, Meredith shook her head sharply. She could control her cravings.

She had to remember what this was all about. Jasmine was going to find a cure. Meredith didn't need access to stolen blood – she needed to be human again.

Jasmine drew blood from Meredith's arm and took a few drops into a pipette to put into a blocky white machine. 'I don't know,' she said, frowning. 'I've separated your blood out in the ultracentrifuge, and I've tried electrophoresis, and analysed it every way I could think of. I can see that there are differences, and I can get some information on how you've changed, but I just don't know what Jack did to make it happen.'

'Doesn't his journal tell you?' Matt asked, picking up the leather-bound book and flipping through its pages. Damon had lent it to Jasmine to help with her research.

Jasmine's mouth scrunched. 'It's big on the effects he observed, but he doesn't really detail the exact procedures he used to get there. It's not a scientific journal.'

'I'm sorry I don't remember more,' Meredith told her. 'But it was all like a dream. He injected me with hypodermics, and it took several nights. I think I was under pretty strong sedation, but sometimes I'd wake up and see him standing over me.' Meredith shuddered. 'Some of the injections went in at the base of my skull, he wasn't lying about that, and some went into my arm. And he operated. I remember a scalpel, and other medical instruments.' Matt was staring at her in horror.

Jasmine looked at Meredith apologetically. 'I can keep running the same tests, and see if there's something I missed. But I'm not sure how much I'm going to find.' Her eyes shone with tears.

'I understand—' Meredith began, but Matt was already moving forward to wrap his arms around Jasmine.

'It's OK,' he said, pressing Jasmine's head against his shoulder. 'We won't give up.'

Meredith stood back and watched them, feeling uncomfortably out of place as Matt lightly kissed the side of Jasmine's head. Their hearts were beating in time, she could hear them, a steady rhythm.

Was she ever going to be like that again? Would she and Alaric, who she loved so much, ever be simple and wholly human together?

Probably not. Meredith swallowed hard, tasting bitterness. She wasn't going to let herself think that way. Jasmine and Bonnie. Science and magic. Maybe they could fix her, make her herself again.

She had to get out of there. Muttering a quick excuse, she swung out of the room, past their startled faces.

Keeping herself carefully to human speed, Meredith made her way towards the hospital exit. She could smell warm, fresh blood all around her, and her throat felt dry and tight. She walked a little faster.

Bursting out through the doors into the hospital parking lot, Meredith realised she was panting. The sun was shining brightly, and she squinted against the glare. She'd go to her car and go out to the woods and drink from a bird or a rabbit, she decided. She needed blood. Without it, she was weak and dizzy, and her emotions were swooping out of control. She felt like crying all the time.

At the far end of the parking lot, there was someone leaning against her car.

Jack.

Meredith slid her hand into her pocket and wrapped it around the cool wood of a stake, her heart pounding. If she could stake Jack, get him down long enough to snap his neck, maybe she could capture him.

Or maybe he was going to kill her first.

He had seen her, was watching her calmly. There was no point in running away, even if she wanted to. Meredith walked slowly across the parking lot towards him. She felt weirdly relaxed. Maybe she was going to die now. Did it matter? Really, she was already dead, wasn't she? In all the ways that counted.

'I'm not going to hurt you,' Jack said when she got close enough. He held his hands out, loose and open, non-threatening.

'Oh, yeah?' Meredith halted a few feet away from him. 'Good to know.'

'I worked far too hard on you to just waste it all.' The

corners of Jack's eyes crinkled as he gave his familiar affable grin. 'Plus, I'm rather fond of you, despite your betrayal.'

Something inside Meredith curdled, thick and sour. He was fond of her? Jack had destroyed her.

'So, let me make you a deal.' Jack boosted himself up to sit on the hood of Meredith's car, perfectly relaxed. 'Bring me Damon Salvatore and I'll forgive you. The whole thing, erased. You can come back to us, back where you belong. You know living with humans isn't working.'

Meredith froze, glaring at him. Did Jack really think that, after everything, she wanted to be one of them?

Jack paused, looking at her with his bright, inquisitive brown eyes, and then shook his head. 'Take the deal, Meredith,' he said. 'If you don't, I'll come after your friends. I always get what I want.'

'Go to hell,' Meredith snarled. She clutched the stake in her pocket and gauged the distance between them, her muscles tensing. He was so relaxed on the car's hood, not alert to danger. If she moved fast enough . . .

Jack smiled at her, his big, beautiful, warm smile. 'Go to hell?' he echoed, his tone light. 'This whole world is hell, Meredith, you should know that by now. The only choice is whether you're a demon or a victim.'

His grin widened, and he leaned back on his hands, turning his face up to the sun. 'You know which side you're on, don't you?'

Now. Yanking the stake from her pocket, Meredith lunged at him.

And suddenly Jack moved so fast that all she saw was a blur. Her hair lifted in the breeze as he passed.

He was gone.

CHAPTER

23

*D*ear Diary,

I shouldn't be enjoying anything about this.

We're in serious trouble. Jack won't stop sending his vampires after us until either we kill him or he kills Damon. He's powerful and relentless, and I know how intelligent he is – he fooled us all.

When I close my eyes, sometimes I see Damon falling, a stake through his chest, and it feels so real. I can see the pain in the tight lines of Damon's body, the blood streaming from the wound. Agony rips through me – I'm losing something I thought was mine, that I thought was for ever.

It feels just like when Stefan died.

Our search for Siobhan is the slenderest of leads. I should be panicking. Damon is in terrible danger.

And I should be grieving for Stefan just as hard as I was a month ago.

Nothing has changed. If anything, things have gotten worse.

And yet . . .

Elena glanced up from her journal towards the driver's seat.

Damon was driving, his long, strong fingers curled around the wheel, his dark eyes fixed on the horizon. He was so beautiful, Elena thought, examining the fine bones under his flawless pale skin, the soft curve of his mouth, the straight line of his nose. He glanced at her and his lips curled into a brief smile before his eyes went back to the road. A pulse of affection went through the bond between them, and Elena wasn't sure who it had come from.

Damon hums when he doesn't know I'm listening, she wrote, turning back to her journal. *Tunes I don't recognise, dances and holy music from the long centuries he lived in Europe, but other things, too: the ballet music Margaret dances to, old Beatles songs, pop from the radio.*

Even though he technically died centuries ago, Damon's more alive than most people. I remember what Stefan said, back when he first told me their story.

After they rose and realised what they had become, Stefan ran, horrified, far beyond the city gates, preying on animals for fear of harming humans. Damon joined a band of mercenaries, fighting his way across Europe, drinking human blood amid the slaughter and confusion of battle.

Stefan made the noble choice. Damon was wicked, then. But Stefan held himself apart from humanity, caring too much to endanger them by coming close. Damon was right there in the thick of it, always, and it's kept him almost human, tangled up with our warm bodies and complicated, messy emotions.

I loved Stefan so much, with all my heart. I still love him. I'll never stop.

Damon is flawed and quick-tempered and selfish. He's as likely to do the wrong thing as he is the right one.

Damon and I are more alike than Stefan and I ever were. I'm spoiled and headstrong and I want everyone to fall in line with my plans. The worst things anyone ever said about me are sometimes true.

And despite everything – despite Jack, and poor Meredith, and everyone depending on the slimmest chance that we're following the right lead here – I'm having fun. It feels easy and natural, gliding along the roads together, hunting for Siobhan together.

This isn't the first time we've travelled like this. When Stefan was missing, imprisoned in the Dark Dimension, we looked for him together.

But then, Stefan was waiting for me. And now, he's gone. We're going to avenge Stefan, not save him. It's too late for that.

Elena's breath hitched, and she tightened her jaw.

She wasn't going to cry again, not now. Out of the corner of her eye, she saw Damon glance towards her and then his hand, cool and reassuring, brushed her shoulder. Elena sniffed and looked back down at her journal.

Would it be so wrong? If Damon and I stopped fighting these feelings we've always had for each other?

I made up my mind. I chose Stefan and I've never regretted it.

But now he's gone, and I'm going to live for ever. *Alone for ever. I can't help panicking every time I think of it.*

I could turn to Damon. I'm not going to lie to myself about that. I can have him, if I want him. If I stopped holding myself back, I could fall into his arms, and I know he'd catch me.

But I don't know if I can. For years, my feelings for Damon tainted what Stefan and I had. It hurt *Stefan that I loved Damon, too.*

Would turning to Damon now be my last, worst betrayal of Stefan?

Elena looked up again. Damon was humming to himself, softly. His eyes, fixed on the road, had a faraway look.

Something in her chest turned over, a tight, uncomfortable feeling. Elena realised that, for maybe the first time ever, she had no idea what she wanted.

'I'm sorry, my dear, I don't have any suggestions.' Mrs Flowers sipped at her tea, holding the delicate china cup carefully. 'Vampires created by science are a little outside my area of expertise. All I can recommend is increasing your use of the protection spells you already know. Try to keep your friends safe.'

Bonnie nodded. It had been a long shot, anyway, expecting her old friend to have a suggestion. But it just felt natural to come back to Fell's Church and ask Mrs Flowers, who had taught her so much of her magic, for advice.

Since Bonnie had broken up with Zander, she'd thrown herself into trying to find a way to help Meredith and to protect them all from Jack and his minions. It had made her feel a little better, helped her to avoid thinking about how empty her apartment was, how empty her big bed was.

How empty her heart was.

Mrs Flowers was looking older and frailer than the last time they had seen each other, Bonnie realised with a pang. Her hand, pale and thin and spotted with age, shook as she placed her cup back on the table. A little tea sloshed into the saucer.

'Now, tell me, Bonnie,' Mrs Flowers said, fixing Bonnie with sharp blue eyes that were not in the least dimmed by age. 'What else is bothering you?'

Bonnie fumbled for a reply. 'Well, Meredith . . .'

'Not Meredith. Meredith's problem is the same as the vampire problem. There's something else.'

Bonnie heard herself give a funny, half-choked

laugh. Mrs. Flowers had always been able to read Bonnie's emotions.

'It's Zander,' she said, as a hot tear ran down her cheek. 'He's left me.'

With that, the dam broke and she burst into sobs. By the time the frantic storm of tears stopped, Bonnie found herself sitting on the floor, her head in Mrs Flowers's lap as the old lady made soft tutting noises and stroked her hair. Mrs Flowers's dress smelled of lavender, and Bonnie couldn't bring herself to care that she was probably staining it with tears and snot – it was amazingly comforting.

'Tell me everything,' Mrs Flowers said, and Bonnie blurted out the whole story: Zander's strange disconnectedness and the way Bonnie had finally confronted him about it; how he had proposed in the warm, fragrant rose garden and how Bonnie had said no, even though it broke her heart. That Zander was gone now, and that Bonnie ached with loneliness without him. That the few werewolves he had left behind to temporarily guard Dalcrest looked away, their faces stony, when they saw her now, and that Bonnie couldn't blame them. Of course they hated her – she'd hurt their Alpha.

'But I had to,' Bonnie said, sitting back on her heels and wiping her eyes. 'Didn't I? I have to put my friends first right now. They need me.'

Mrs Flowers sighed and sat very still for a moment,

gazing off into the distance. Then she rose, resting one hand on the table as she shuffled towards the living room. 'I want to show you something,' she said. 'Wait here.'

After a moment, she returned, a framed picture in hand. Bonnie recognised it as one she'd seen before, sitting on the mantelpiece in the living room. A black-and-white photograph of a handsome young man in uniform. His dark hair was close cropped, and his eyes were pale, probably blue. His face was serious, but there was a natural curve at the corners of his mouth that suggested he had a sense of humour.

'He looks nice,' Bonnie said, scrubbing her hand against her face again. She felt exhausted and longed to just lie down on Mrs Flowers's floor and take a nice long nap. 'Who is he?'

'William Flowers.' Mrs Flowers gazed down at the picture, her smile soft and sad. 'Bill.'

'Your husband?' Bonnie asked, peering at the picture with fresh interest.

Mrs Flowers sighed again, a soft, almost soundless exhalation of breath, and shook her head. 'Not quite, although I took his name,' she said. 'He was my sweetheart. We grew up together and fell in love. It felt like it was meant to be. We laughed so much together, knew each other so well. Understood each other without having to try. I thought we'd go on like that for ever.'

'So what happened?' Bonnie scrambled up off the floor, settling herself into the chair next to her mentor.

'We were engaged. And then he was drafted.' Mrs Flowers passed a hand over her eyes. 'I was so afraid of losing him. He wanted to get married before he went overseas, but I couldn't do it, I couldn't start our married life with him in danger. And then he was killed in action. I lost everything.'

Bonnie gasped. 'I'm so sorry,' she whispered.

Mrs Flowers's wise, calm face crumpled in well-remembered pain. 'I spent years trying to contact him from beyond the veil. I wanted him to know how much I loved him. I tried everything. Séances, working with mediums, wandering the no man's land between the living and the dead, inducing visions . . . nothing worked. Some people, when they die, pass out of our reach.'

'We couldn't reach Stefan,' Bonnie said, feeling achingly sad.

'Come outside with me.' Mrs Flowers rose stiffly and led the way out of the kitchen door into her herb garden, moving more quickly than she had earlier.

It was warm and bright outside, and Bonnie automatically tipped her head backward to feel the sun on her face. Mrs Flowers led her through the winding paths of her herb garden. 'Let's see what you remember,' she said. 'Tell me about this herb bed.'

'Oh. Um.' Bonnie scanned the plants. 'Marjoram.

For healing. And for cooking. Amaranth, also known as love-lies-bleeding. For healing and protection. Celandine, or swallow's wort, for happiness.'

'Very good, I see you haven't abandoned your training. And the bush next to them?'

The bush had long green leaves and cascading purple flowers, each made of a round spray of thin petals. 'Pretty,' Bonnie said. 'But I don't know what it is.'

Mrs Flowers picked one of the blossoms and sniffed it. 'Mimosa, my dear. It's for joy rising from sorrow. Second chances.' Smiling, she passed the flower to Bonnie, and Bonnie automatically brought it up to her face and sniffed. It smelled clean and fresh.

Bonnie held the flower gently, but her heart felt as heavy as a stone. Mrs Flowers had loved her Bill, and despite everything, had lost him anyway. Mimosa or not, it was hard to believe that joy could come from sorrow.

CHAPTER
24

Matt shifted the two full bags of groceries he carried, balancing one against his hip as he dug his key to Jasmine's building out of his pocket.

A little thrill of satisfaction shot through him as he twisted the key in the lock. They'd only exchanged keys last week, and it felt really important, another sign that they were all in, really and truly committed to being part of each other's lives. Jasmine had kissed him hard, her lips firm and sure against his, after she pressed her keys into his palm, and it had been the best moment of a very tough week.

Jasmine had been stressing out. She'd run every test she could think of on Meredith's blood, but was still coming up empty.

He clumped up the stairs, swinging the bags and

thinking about how a nice dinner might help Jasmine feel better. Stuffing the chicken with thyme, lemon and garlic, he thought, would give it a nice flavour. And wine might help her relax. Matt was humming as he reached the top of the stairs and turned towards Jasmine's apartment.

The door was hanging wide open.

Matt dropped his bags, hearing the wine bottle smash, and ran towards it, his heart pounding. He barrelled through the front door and stopped dead, horrified.

Jasmine's living room had been trashed. The velvety-soft sofa was flipped over and disembowelled. The weavings she'd put on the walls were ripped down, her tables knocked over and broken.

'Jasmine?' Matt called, breaking out of his shock. He raced down the hall, checking the other rooms.

The kitchen, bathroom and bedroom were more of the same, everything smashed and broken. The closet door had been ripped off, clothes trailing out as if someone had tried to hold on to them while being yanked out of the closet. 'Jasmine!'

His phone rang. jasmine, the display read. Thank God. She was OK. She would have some explanation. Tension flowed out of him, his shoulders relaxing.

'Where are you?' Matt answered the phone. 'Are you OK?'

A low, warm, familiar chuckle. Not Jasmine's.

Everything went fuzzy around the edges, and Matt swayed on his feet, light-headed. Jack.

'I'm fine,' Jack said. 'Your girlfriend seems a little nervous, though.'

'You –' Matt clenched his teeth, snapping things back into focus. 'I'll kill you if you hurt her,' he spat.

Jack laughed again. 'You can't, can you?' he asked. 'You know, I didn't really get to know Jasmine back when you and I were hanging around together. I can see why you like her. She's pretty tasty, isn't she?' He moved the phone, and Matt heard a soft whimper.

'Jasmine?' he said, straining to hear. 'Honey, be strong. It'll be all right.' His pulse was pounding, his hands sweating. He couldn't think.

'She's fine,' Jack said. 'For now.'

'Please don't hurt her,' Matt said. 'I'll do anything you want.' He felt sick and dizzy. Not Jasmine, he prayed, not good, strong Jasmine, who'd been outside all of this, safe – until Matt brought her in.

'I want Damon,' Jack said, his voice suddenly cold and tight. 'Bring me Damon, and I'll let your girlfriend go.'

CHAPTER

25

'She's got to be somewhere. Siobhan can't have gotten away from us.' Elena had her hands balled into fists, pressed against her temples. She was concentrating hard, her pretty face twisted. 'If I could just find her . . .'

'Calm down,' Damon told her as he steered the car down the highway, still heading north. It seemed as good a direction as any, although Elena had lost Siobhan's trail earlier that day. 'We'll pull into the next motel we see. You need a good night's rest. It'll come back to you.'

The sun was setting, throwing long shadows across the road. If Elena ate and rested, maybe she'd be able to find her Power again.

He was having trouble, too. Anxiety radiated through their bond, making him jittery. Elena was in pain, her head aching, her muscles tense, and that made Damon hurt, too. He longed to pull her against him and stroke her soft golden hair, to press her face against his shoulder and hold her until she calmed.

'We can't stop,' Elena said firmly. 'There's no time.' She leaned back against the window and shut her eyes, making little huffing noises as she drew in breaths through her nose, then let them out through her mouth.

Damon knew she was trying to force her Guardian Powers to the surface. They were strong but fickle, these Powers. Even when she was working on a Guardian task, like now, she couldn't always rely on them.

Ridiculous Celestial Guardians. They wielded huge Powers themselves, more than any vampire or witch, but they meted out tiny bits of Power to the Earthly Guardians like drips from a faucet. Damon had to wonder: did the Celestial Guardians want to keep Earthly Guardians like Elena weak and dependent on them? Or were their own Powers on Earth limited?

In any case, it made no difference now. The important thing was Elena.

'Listen,' he said, and reached out to stroke her arm, gently reassuring her. 'You're strong as hell, princess. The strongest person I've ever met. You'll do this stubborn and bull-headed, just like you've done everything else the whole time I've known you.'

He gave her his most blinding grin, and something softened in Elena's eyes. They stared at each other for a long moment, her gaze so deeply blue, as blue as the lapis lazuli that let Damon walk in sunlight.

Something in his chest tightened, and he felt it tug towards Elena, as sure as a magnet. They were breathing in time, he realised, their chests rising and falling in perfect accord. He couldn't resist her any more.

He didn't want to resist. Elena was all he wanted, all he needed. She had been since the first time he saw her, a pretty high school girl in the morning sunshine, all pink and gold and flushed with the warmth of life. Or, since the first time his mind brushed hers, and he realised she was more than that: strong and fierce, stubborn and proud. Perfect for him.

Slowly, giving her time to pull away, Damon slid closer. Elena didn't back away, but held his gaze, her blue eyes almost challenging. She wanted this, he could feel that want burning through their bond. Gently, holding his breath, he pressed his lips to hers.

Her lips were impossibly soft and warm, the softest thing he'd ever felt. Damon's eyes closed and he leaned closer, cupping her cheek with one hand. The connection between them throbbed with hot energy, with desire. His fingers tangled in her silky hair, and he pulled her closer still.

He could feel their auras blending. It was as if they were melting into each other. He could almost see them, the way Elena had described their auras to him, his peacock blue and rust red, hers a soft gold. They were entwining – he could feel it. They were stronger like this, better together.

Damon thought briefly of his brother, then pushed the thought away. Stefan was gone. And Damon and Elena remained. He stroked Elena's cheek, ran his hand over her shoulders, down her arm. She was his, he knew it as surely as he'd ever known anything. They belonged to each other.

And then, a sharp, hard jerk. All over, he felt exposed, strained. Something pulled at him, a brisk, insistent tug.

With a muffled gasp against Elena's mouth, Damon realised she was drawing his aura into hers, his peacock blue slowly shading to gold. Her aura was growing bigger, brighter.

It hurt a little, but it was somehow thrilling. The steady, draining pull made him light-headed, made him sigh against her lips. Was this how it felt for her when he'd fed on her?

Just as when he'd fed on her, this was love, he was sure of it.

Damon tangled both hands in Elena's hair, silken strands between his fingers, and tried to push his aura towards her, to give her whatever she needed.

Elena pulled away slowly and Damon sat back, drained and relaxed. His head was swimming. They stared at each other, and Elena licked her lips quickly, just a brief slide of her tongue.

'West,' she said.

'What?' Damon asked. His heart was pounding, slow and heavy, and it was an effort to speak.

'I see it now,' Elena said. 'She went west.'

Shaking himself back into alertness, Damon started the engine. 'We can turn west on I-64,' he said, his mouth dry. 'About half a mile.'

'Good,' Elena said. She was looking straight ahead through the windshield. Damon checked the connection between them, but Elena was locked down tight. All he got was an intent concentration on the road ahead. Whatever else she was thinking, she wasn't letting herself feel it, not yet. She wasn't going to let him in.

Tentatively, he reached across the seat between them, his hand palm up, waiting for her hand to clasp his.

Elena did not take his hand.

CHAPTER

26

Matt wiped his sweaty palms against his jeans, and let his head rest against the driver's seat for a moment. He took a deep breath before looking at the polished wooden stave in the passenger seat – one of Meredith's old bo staffs. He gritted his teeth and picked it up. It was cool and sturdy in his hands, and he gripped it tightly, trying to remember all the moves Meredith had ever taught him.

Then he climbed out of the car, dread pooling in his stomach. Waiting wasn't going to make this any easier.

Gravel scattered under his feet as he made his way across the parking lot towards Jack's warehouse. Everything was silent; no signs of life in the empty lot. The silence seemed wrong, and after a moment Matt realised how weirdly complete it was: no sounds of traffic from the highway, no rustling of leaves from the trees, no birdsong. He shuddered, but kept walking.

Matt couldn't wait for the others to make a plan, couldn't wait for Elena and Damon to come home. Not while Jasmine was suffering.

Sweet, intelligent Jasmine with her shining eyes and softly curving mouth. Jasmine who loved him, who trusted him. Who had thrown herself wholeheartedly into trying to help Matt and his friends. Whatever happened, he had to at least try to save her. Tears prickled at the back of Matt's eyes, and he blinked them away.

He wasn't an idiot. There was a nest of vampires inside this warehouse. With his total lack of special powers, he was probably going to his death.

Matt swallowed hard. It would be better to die today trying to save Jasmine than to live sixty more years knowing he'd abandoned her.

Clutching the stave tightly, he considered his silent surroundings. The whole place seemed still and empty, as if it were deserted, but Matt knew better. He inspected the door. There was a little rust on its panels, but it was solid-looking and made of steel. There was no way he'd be able to kick it down.

With a mental shrug, Matt raised his fist and pounded heavily on the door, which let out metallic echoing thuds. They were vampires; they would have heard him coming.

The door gave a long screech as a lanky dark-haired guy with close-set eyes – not a guy, a vampire – opened it. Acting on instinct, Matt moved fast.

One hard thrust from the stave in Matt's hand, and the vampire staggered and fell, blood blooming red across his chest, his mouth open in a grimace of surprise. His eyes dimmed. He was dead, at least for the moment. Lucky hit. Matt knew with deadly certainty that his luck wasn't going to last.

Matt stepped over the dead vampire and moved towards the next one, a slim blonde girl with a short swinging bob.

She was just standing still, looking bewildered, as if events were happening too quickly for her to catch up. Beyond her, chained to the back wall of the warehouse, he glimpsed Jasmine and quickly looked away, his breath catching.

He couldn't concentrate on the fight if he looked at her right now. He wouldn't have much time before the vampires got over their surprise and their superior reflexes kicked in.

But maybe he could get past one more, maybe he could make his way to Jasmine. *Please*, he prayed silently, raising his stave again. *Please. If I'm going to die, at least let me touch Jasmine again.*

But as he moved towards the girl, a pair of strong arms, as unyielding as steel bands, wrapped around him from behind and pinned Matt's arms to his sides.

He tried to struggle, but it was pointless; however much he strained, he couldn't move at all. Out of the corner of his eye, he saw the tall, thin vampire struggling to his feet, already beginning to recover. Giving in to despair, Matt sagged against his captor's arms.

'Can you think of a reason I shouldn't kill you right now?' Jack's voice said, soft and low. His breath was warm against Matt's ear, and Matt shuddered.

Jack squeezed him tighter, and Matt struggled to breathe. It was painful, the pressure of Jack's arms compressing his ribs, slowly pressing the air from his lungs. Now that the fight was over, and he'd failed, just as he'd feared he would, he let himself look across the warehouse towards Jasmine for the first time.

Her arms were chained high above her head, her muscles taut with the strain, and she was looking straight back at him, her eyes shining with love. Tears ran down her cheeks, making long tracks through the dirt there. There were streaks of dried blood on the side of her throat. She gave Matt a tiny, tremulous smile, and his chest ached. He hadn't saved her, and now she was trying to send him comfort.

'Take me instead,' Matt blurted out.

'What?' Jack sounded startled, and his arms loosened a fraction. Matt gasped in a quick breath.

'I'm better for your purposes than Jasmine is,' he said hurriedly. This was his only back-up plan, Jasmine's only chance. He had to sell it. 'I'm a better hostage.

Elena and the others have known me longer, they're more likely to trade Damon for me. You hunted with us. You know what I'm saying is true.'

Jack made a thoughtful humming noise in his throat, considering, and Matt clenched his teeth. This was the only way he could possibly save Jasmine, he realised, by throwing himself into the abyss. They were all watching him, five or six vampires, their eyes hostile. Everything was sharp and bright at the edges, and he wondered if he was going into shock.

Then Jack huffed, a short, amused sound. 'Who says chivalry is dead?'

Fast enough so that the world blurred around him, Matt felt himself lifted and rushed across the warehouse. Jack slammed him back against the wall so hard that Matt was knocked breathless once more.

'Now, tell me why I shouldn't keep you both?' Jack asked.

Matt felt sick. Jack wouldn't really keep them both, would he? He gulped quickly, nervously. He had to think. 'Jasmine has to tell the others what happened,' he said. 'You won't get Damon if they don't need to trade for me. And you won't get Damon if they think you can't be trusted to trade me back. If you let her go, it'll be a show of good faith.'

Jack pursed his lips thoughtfully. 'Good point. Sadie, get over here and unlock the cuffs.'

The blonde girl hurried over and took the cuffs off

Jasmine's wrists, pulling her away from the wall. Jasmine was shaking, hard, and she reached out for Matt, her hands trembling. 'Please . . .' she said, her voice strained. 'Let me talk to him.'

Jack shoved Matt roughly into the place where Jasmine had been and began to lock the cuffs around his wrists, yanking his arms up with a vicious twist that made his shoulders burn. Matt grunted with pain. 'Better get out while you can, sweetheart,' Jack said indifferently, and pushed her away. 'Sadie, take her home.'

As Sadie began to pull her away, Matt took one last look at Jasmine. Her beautiful liquid brown eyes were full of tears. Trying to fill his own gaze with all of his love and all the confidence he didn't feel, Matt told her, 'It's all right. I'll see you soon.'

Jasmine's fingers brushed over his arm, featherlight, as Sadie pulled her away. At least they had touched one last time.

CHAPTER 27

'This is it,' Elena said, her mouth dry and her hands twitching with anticipation. Siobhan's trail had led them westward, high into the foothills of the Appalachian Mountains. And now, here they were, staring at a small cave entrance.

Elena bent to look more closely. A long cavern stretched further than she could see. They'd have to crawl to get through it. Elena cringed at the thought of moving into the damp and darkness, the heavy stone pressing down all around them.

But they didn't have a choice. Siobhan's blood-red aura, the colour of death and violence, led straight into the cave. Despite her reluctance to crawl into the dark, Elena's Guardian Powers were straining inside her, urging her forward. There was someone evil here, someone she was duty-bound to destroy.

No. Elena closed her eyes for a second and willed herself calm. She had to remember that they weren't planning to kill Siobhan, not yet. Not until they had found out what she knew about Jack.

'I'll go first,' Damon said. Elena opened her mouth to argue and he raised an eyebrow at her challengingly.

Just then Elena's phone rang. JASMINE, the display told her. Elena frowned. Jasmine never called her. Still, maybe it was good news about her research on Meredith's blood.

'Hello?' she said, picking up. Immediately, she tensed.

Jasmine was crying, harsh sobs coming through the phone. Not good news, after all. 'Jasmine? What is it? What's happened?' Beside Elena, Damon stiffened.

'Jack has Matt,' Jasmine said, her voice rough and panicked. 'He wants to trade him for Damon. He – it's horrible, Elena. They're feeding on him, and he's only there because of me.'

For a moment, Elena froze. Not Matt. He was brave and strong, but he didn't have special Power or protection, not like she did. Not like Damon did, or Bonnie, or Meredith.

Not like Stefan had, and Elena's stomach knotted as the picture of Stefan falling, his expression of shock fading into blankness, flashed through her mind again. There was no way Matt could survive Jack, not if Stefan hadn't.

Damon took the phone out of her hand. He'd heard everything, of course. 'We'll get your boyfriend back,' he said soothingly into the phone. 'Once we take care of business here, find out the best way to handle Jack, we'll be right there.' He paused to listen to Jasmine's reply, but Elena couldn't hear what she said. 'They won't kill him,' he said after a moment, his eyes meeting Elena's. 'Not if Jack wants to trade him for me.'

After he hung up, Damon looked at Elena again, his dark eyes unreadable. He'd been looking at her like that a lot, ever since they'd kissed a few hours ago. Unthinkingly, Elena touched her lips, and felt herself flush as Damon's gaze lingered on her fingers.

'We'd better get moving,' he said abruptly. 'It appears that your friends can't keep themselves out of trouble for even a couple of days without us.' Crouching down, he contemplated the cave entrance for a moment.

Something about the high defensive line of Damon's shoulders, the pale skin at the nape of his neck made Elena say impulsively, 'We wouldn't trade you, Damon. Not even for Matt.'

Damon looked back over his shoulder at her and flashed a brief, brilliant smile. 'Good to know.' Ducking his head, he crawled through the mouth of the cavern. Pulling out the flashlight she carried, Elena followed.

The stone was cold and rough against her hands and knees, and it was difficult to hold on to the flashlight, which showed her little more than Damon's heels. He could see in the dark as well as a cat, Elena knew, but her own view was restricted to the small pool of light thrown by her flashlight, and the red strands of Siobhan's aura, strands as thick as Elena's wrist, leading her steadily on.

Just as Elena began to feel that she couldn't take the sensation of the stone walls pressing in on her from every direction, the tunnel opened up into a wider cavern. She straightened up with relief, her back and legs aching from the long crawl.

Siobhan wasn't in this part of the cave, either, she realised immediately. The blood-red trail of her aura led further on, disappearing through another opening in the rock wall. Elena stood shoulder-to-shoulder with Damon, scanning the cavern with her flashlight.

The stone walls were rough and dark, glittering in places with mica, maybe, or fool's gold. It was damp and cold – they must have come a good way underground.

'I smell blood,' Damon said, very quietly. 'Human blood. Which way does the trail lead?' Elena pointed, and he nodded grimly.

Walking softly, their arms brushing, they followed the blood-red aura. Something was pushing eagerly inside Elena – *find her, finish her, eliminate her* – but she concentrated on keeping her Powers under control. *Don't attack unless you have to*, she told herself. The

Guardians wanted Siobhan dead, but Elena needed her alive.

They stepped through an opening in the rock wall, and Elena instinctively flinched backward, grabbing hold of Damon's arm to steady herself.

Corpses were littered carelessly across the smooth stone floor, tumbled on top of each other like dolls dropped by a bored child, ten or twelve of them, all dead. Closest to Elena's feet, an elderly woman stared up through empty eyes, her throat torn out.

Surrounded by the bodies stood a tall figure in a long, bloodstained white dress. Black hair flowed around her, twining over her shoulders and down to her waist. Siobhan. In her arms, half-wrapped in Siobhan's hair, was another victim, Siobhan's teeth working busily at his throat. Her eyes were closed.

Kill her. Elena started forward, all her strategies forgotten in the need to stop Siobhan, to protect her victim. Dangerous. Evil. Her Guardian Power bubbled up in her chest, ready to attack. Damon's hand gripped her shoulder, trying to hold her back.

But they were too late. As soon as Elena moved, Siobhan's eyes shot open, vividly blue, even in the shadowy light of the flashlight. She dropped the man she'd been feeding on, and he landed with a thud on the stone floor of the cave. He was clearly dead.

The heat in Elena's chest dissipated, leaving an empty ache. There was no one to save here.

Siobhan's eyes, gleaming with wicked joy, fixed on Elena. Her lips were red and slick with blood. 'You . . .' she said, her voice a hoarse whisper. 'I dreamed of you.' Her gaze flickered to Damon. 'And a little vampire, too.'

Elena felt Damon stiffen, and she shushed him with a touch on his arm. 'We've been looking for you, Siobhan,' she said politely. 'We came to ask for your help.'

Moving faster than Elena could track, Siobhan was suddenly terribly close. Elena struggled for breath, realizing only after a moment that Siobhan's hand was tight around her throat. She was so fast.

Damon snarled, and Elena sent him a warning through their bond: wait. Siobhan wasn't hurting Elena. Not yet, anyway. And they needed her to listen to them.

Now that she was holding Elena, Siobhan was curiously still. Her eyes searched Elena's. 'You're very . . .' she said, sounding puzzled and distant, like a sleepwalker. She looked Elena up and down. '. . . shiny. Gold. Not quite human. I don't know what you are.'

Elena concentrated on breathing, slow and shallow. She needed to stay calm. Siobhan's fingers were strong on her throat, and up close the old vampire smelled like fresh blood, like death.

She can't kill you, Elena told herself firmly, and kept her eyes steady on Siobhan's. Her Guardian instincts squirmed inside her: *kill her, kill her now*, and Elena firmly restrained herself. She wouldn't kill Siobhan, not yet. Not while she might be of use to them.

'Jack Daltry,' Damon said, watching them closely. 'He's killing vampires, like you and me. We want to kill him first. Can you help us?'

Siobhan grinned savagely, and Elena recoiled. The vampire's canines were fully extended, stained with blood. Smiling, any illusion of humanity ripped away from her face. She looked like a monster. 'That's not even his name,' she said. 'What chance do you have, knowing nothing? Idiots.'

'Henrik Goetsch, then,' Damon said, and Siobhan's eyes widened slightly. She hadn't expected them to know Jack's real name.

'Henrik Goetsch,' she said thoughtfully, rolling the name over her tongue as if she was tasting it. 'Yes, I remember Henrik.' Abruptly, she let go of Elena's throat and strode away, her bare foot stepping on a corpse's hand as nonchalantly as if it had been a twig. The edge of her long gown dragged through a pool of blood.

Elena sucked in a deep draught of air, her hand on her throat. 'What do you remember about him?' she asked, keeping her voice steady.

Siobhan swung around to face them. For a moment, she looked stricken, her eyes huge and unhappy, and then she laughed harshly. 'He's not a nice man, little sunshine,' she said.

'What did he do?' Elena asked softly. She smiled

hesitantly at Siobhan – *you can tell me, we're just two girls* – and the vampire's eyes narrowed.

'Trapped me,' she said bitterly. 'Tricked me. Pretended to love me. He took so much blood, and he wouldn't let me feed.' Her lips curled into a smile. 'I got loose, though, and killed his lab assistant. He wasn't expecting that.' She licked her lips, reminiscing, and then scowled. 'She tasted horrible, though. All wrong. Killed Henrik's girlfriend, too.'

Satisfaction began to uncurl inside Elena, and she could feel the same emotion coming from Damon through their bond. They had been right. Siobhan was the vampire Jack had used to make his artificial vampires.

'Don't you want revenge?' Damon asked, stepping towards Siobhan, his hands held out as if he was coaxing a skittish animal. 'Don't you want to kill Henrik? Can he be killed?'

'Oh, I'll kill him one of these days,' Siobhan said, idly wandering among her corpses. She toed a middle-aged man over with her bare foot, so that he flopped on to his back, staring with empty eyes at the roof of the cave. Siobhan smiled down at him, as if she was laughing at a private joke. 'I leave these bodies where I know he's been. To remind him I know his secret, and that I'm coming for him.'

'His secret?' Elena said breathlessly. 'So he can be killed.'

Siobhan looked coyly at them through her lashes and mimed zipping her lips. One of the smudges of blood on her face was definitely a handprint, Elena realised, feeling a little sick.

Siobhan cocked her head to one side, considering. 'I knew Henrik would leave himself a back door. He wouldn't create an army he couldn't get rid of,' she said slowly. 'So I watched and waited – I was very clever about it – and eventually I found out there was a poison that would kill the vampires he'd made. And I stole it.'

'It'll kill Henrik, too?' Damon asked swiftly.

'Of course,' Siobhan said. 'He's just like the rest of them.' She wandered closer to them, her blue eyes fixed on Elena. With a thrill of disgust, Elena realised she was eyeing the vein on the side of Elena's throat. 'I'm not convinced I should let you have it, though. I don't *want* anyone else getting my revenge. Maybe I should kill you instead. Eliminate the competition.'

An instinctual fear clenched Elena's muscles. *She can't kill you. But she could hurt you trying.* This old, wicked vampire had dragged so many victims deep underground and killed them all, just to prove a point. She was strong, and determined.

'Please,' Elena said softly. She felt oddly as if she was rolling over to show her own underbelly, appeasing the vicious old vampire. 'We need to kill Jack now. We want the same thing you do.' Her Guardian instincts were chanting *kill her kill her now*, but Elena swallowed them back and smiled at the vampire.

The edges of Siobhan's lips curled up in a smile, and her eyes gleamed with triumph. 'Take me with you.'

Damon shot Elena a look. His distrust of Siobhan came clearly through their bond.

Elena hesitated, and Siobhan's smile widened. 'Take me with you,' she said again. 'The only way you're getting the poison is if I can watch Henrik die.'

Damon was right, they couldn't trust her. But they didn't have a choice, not if they wanted Siobhan's secret. She swallowed hard and said, as evenly as she could, 'OK. Let's go.'

As they headed for the exit, Damon's eyes met Elena's. She could feel the same apprehension bubbling through them both. Siobhan was clearly vicious and unstable. What kind of ally would she be?

For now, they needed her. But as soon as Jack was dead, Elena promised inwardly, soothing her restless Guardian Power, she would kill Siobhan herself.

CHAPTER 28

The drive back had been far too long, Damon thought, even though they'd taken a straight route home instead of the wandering path that had led them to the caverns. In the back seat, Siobhan had grumbled constantly, complaining about the movement of the car, the confined space, the smells of gasoline and oil.

For his part, Damon had hardly been able to stand the smell of drying blood from her face and clothing. It made his teeth ache with hunger.

'It's almost daylight,' she said now, as Damon took the side road that would lead them to Jack's warehouse lair. 'If the sun reaches inside this car, I'll be sure to bring you both down with me.' Her tilted pale eyes were commanding, staring at his reflection in the rear-view mirror.

'We'll be in before dawn, and the warehouse doesn't have any windows,' he told her reassuringly. 'We can cover you with something to get you out after Jack's dead.'

That would be a good way to kill her, he mused. A quick shove into the sunlight, a protecting blanket ripped away, and they'd be free of Siobhan before she could turn on them. He glanced at Elena, wondering if she'd caught the image through their bond.

But Elena was leaning forward, peering through the windshield at the warehouse. 'Good, they're already here.'

The others were waiting in a parking lot across the highway from Jack's warehouse, far enough away that Jack's vampires wouldn't be able to hear them coming. Meredith, tall and poised, stood half concealed in the shadows, her eyes shining in the reflected glare of their headlights. As the car turned into the lot, she raised a hand in greeting. Beside her was Alaric, his hands crammed into his pockets. A little behind them, Damon glimpsed two curly heads. Bonnie and Jasmine.

No Zander, no Pack. His little redbird had seemed strained the last time he saw her; there must be trouble in paradise. It was a pity. They could have used the wolves.

Damon dismissed the thought. They'd work with what they had. He parked the car, and he and Elena crossed the parking lot to their friends, Siobhan stalking behind them. There was a cold feeling on the back of Damon's neck. He didn't like not being able to see Siobhan's every move.

'What a lot of humans,' Siobhan said. 'Will we feed before we kill Jack?'

'No,' Damon said firmly, and the older vampire gave an exaggerated sigh of disappointment.

'Jack's in there,' Meredith said, as soon as they got close, jerking her head towards the warehouse on the other side of the highway.

'Oh, she's one of Henrik's nasty creations,' Siobhan said, sounding disgusted. 'She's not even real.' Meredith's hand clenched on her stave.

Damon shook his head, and Meredith loosened her grip. She looked pale and drawn, which answered one question he'd had. She hadn't been drinking human blood, not since she came back from Jack's group. He hadn't had anything but animal blood either, not since he'd fed from Elena. Neither of them were going to be at their best for this fight.

Still, they just had to overpower Jack long enough to inject him with the poison. And to rescue Matt, Damon supposed.

'Give me the poison,' he said, holding his hand out to Siobhan. She cocked her eyebrow at him. 'Please.' She hesitated for a moment and then reached into her pocket and drew out a vial of dark liquid. She'd had it hidden somewhere at the back of the cave among her corpses. She hadn't let them see exactly where.

Damon waited. Siobhan turned the vial over in her hands, watching the liquid flow back and forth. Her eyes were hooded and thoughtful.

She's not going to hand it over. Damon sighed inwardly, preparing himself for the fight. Siobhan, freshly full of human blood, would be stronger than he was, but at least she was outnumbered.

'I don't know,' Siobhan said slowly. 'I've been waiting a long time to kill Henrik. And it was very clever of me to find the poison. This is mine.'

'Please,' Elena said. 'Siobhan, you've been following him for so long. It must be a burden. Let us help you.'

The two pairs of blue eyes met squarely, and Damon was reminded of generals on a battlefield. They weren't friends, would never be friends, but they had a common cause.

Siobhan broke their exchanged gaze first. With a scornful curl of her lip, she gave Damon the vial, her fingers cool as they brushed against his.

He looked at Jasmine. 'Did you bring a syringe?' Jasmine nodded and bent her head to look through the medical bag she carried.

Damon prepared the syringe and tucked it carefully into his shirt pocket before turning to the others. 'Ready?'

Everyone nodded. The humans each gripped a stake, while Meredith stood beside Damon. Her lips curled back in a snarl, showing her canines, already sharp and long.

'Breaking their necks will keep them down longest,' Damon told them, 'but that's tough for a human to manage. Strike hard and keep moving.' He shot Elena a small smile. She would be fine, he reminded himself. Nothing supernatural could kill her.

'Damon and I will go after Jack,' she said. 'Everyone else needs to focus on Matt. Jasmine, you know where he is?'

Jasmine nodded, her eyes huge. 'They have him chained up against the back wall.'

'I can break the chains,' Meredith said quickly. 'Just be careful everybody, OK?'

Bonnie and Alaric linked their free hands, beginning to murmur a protective charm. Damon glanced at them all, the brave little group of humans – plus Meredith – he'd somehow gotten himself entangled with, and felt oddly fond. He could count on them to fight, to protect each other until their last breaths. Behind them, Siobhan stood statue still, her pale face blank, the splotches of blood on her dress dry now.

'Are you with us?' Damon demanded.

She stared at him. 'I'm coming,' she said in her throaty, expressionless voice.

'Let's go, then,' Damon said, and they crossed the highway.

Jack's vampires depended too much on their

deadbolts and their sharp hearing to protect them, Damon thought with disgust. When he picked the lock and swung the door quietly open, they caught the guards on duty by surprise. They were a young couple, still almost human, who'd been wrapped up in each other instead of watching for intruders.

Damon had the impression of a bewildered, young face as he snapped the neck of the guy. When he turned to take care of the girl, Meredith already had her down on the floor.

'Good work,' Damon muttered, and Meredith rolled her eyes.

'Come on,' she said softly, and Jasmine, Bonnie, and Alaric followed her further into the warehouse. There were crates piled everywhere, and they were soon out of sight, although Damon could hear their footsteps. He frowned. If he could hear them, so could any other vampire.

Elena stood beside him, poised with a stake ready in her hand. A little behind her, Siobhan, cold-eyed and expressionless, walked across the girl vampire's body, a rib snapping audibly beneath her feet. Damon repressed a shudder. He didn't like her so close behind Elena, looming like an angel of death.

Turning his attention, Damon scanned the warehouse for Jack, keeping his eyes and ears open. 'Over there,' he murmured, jerking his chin towards a stack of crates. There was someone behind them.

He cocked an eyebrow at Elena, and she nodded.

A grunt came from the other side of the warehouse, and he glanced over just in time to see another vampire fall, Alaric's stake in his chest. They needed to find Jack, kill him and get out, before his minions started recovering and they lost their advantage.

Senses on alert, Damon rounded the crates. Through his shirt pocket, he could feel the hypodermic needle.

A warm body slammed into his, kicking and punching, and he raised a hand to protect the syringe. His left hand cupping his pocket, he spun and kicked his attacker away. It was only another of Jack's vampires, a round-faced blonde. Damon snapped his neck with his free hand without pausing.

'Use your teeth, idiot,' he muttered. He didn't know how Jack chose his minions, but it wasn't for their brains. Or, Meredith excepted, their fighting skill.

A voice came from behind him. 'I've been looking forward to this.'

Damon turned. Jack was lightly poised on the balls of his feet, his eyes tracking Damon's every move. He wasn't underestimating Damon as an opponent, not any more.

With a burst of energy, Damon charged, canines extended. He slammed into Jack and they both fell heavily to the floor.

Sinking his teeth into Jack's throat, Damon grappled with him, trying to keep him down as the strange taste of Jack's blood filled his mouth. Damon grimaced in disgust, but kept biting, working his teeth back and forth in Jack's throat to reopen the wound before it had time to heal. Jack grunted in pain and thrashed beneath Damon's weight, but Damon had him pinned.

The chemical-laden blood was flooding into his mouth, and Damon swallowed rapidly, gulping it down despite the taste. Blood would make him stronger, and he desperately needed that if he was going to defeat Jack. Damon felt almost light-headed with it, fireworks bursting behind his eyes.

Damon drew back to get his hands on the syringe, pulling his canines from Jack's neck. Jack twisted and thrashed, bucking up and finally throwing Damon off. Damon rolled backward, crashing into the crate behind him.

Jack leapt to his feet in one smooth, controlled motion, his face twisted with rage. Then he froze, looking past Damon. 'Siobhan?' he asked. There was a note of fear in his voice, the first Damon had ever heard from him.

'Hello, Jack.' Siobhan's voice came from behind, cool and mocking, but Damon didn't turn to look at her. This was his chance.

He pulled the syringe from his pocket. The liquid inside shimmered dark blue in the light of the warehouse. He began to inch towards Jack.

Jack suddenly gave a cut-off shout as his body flew

backward like a rag doll's and slammed into the warehouse wall. Suspended there, his feet dangled above the floor. His hands were pressed backward, flat against the wall. He was straining, the tendons in his neck visibly taut. He couldn't move.

For a moment, Damon was stunned into stillness himself. Then he felt Elena's concentration, her triumph coming through the bond. Being near Siobhan must have woken up her Powers. Damon glanced at Elena. Her hands were up, palms out, as if she was holding Jack in place, and her eyes were bright with intensity.

'Give it to me. I want to do it,' Elena muttered, and Damon snapped back into action.

He took two steps towards her and slapped the syringe into her palm. Let Elena have this kill. If finishing Jack would give her some peace, help her find solace for Stefan's murder, then Damon would gladly give it to her.

Still holding Jack in place, Elena stepped forward and jammed the needle into Jack's neck. As she pushed the plunger on the hypodermic, she smiled, a sharp, angry smile – no joy in it, but a great deal of satisfaction. From behind them, Siobhan began to laugh.

Jack blinked. And then he began to struggle, his head banging back against the wall and his arms coming up to grasp at Elena. Her hold on him must be slipping.

Damon ran forward and tackled him away, ripping his hands off Elena. They fell to the ground together and rolled, Jack tearing at Damon with hands and teeth. He was as strong as ever.

It hadn't worked, Damon realised, filling with heavy dread, as he felt blood run down his side. It hadn't worked. Damon slammed Jack's head against the concrete floor and snarled with rage and frustration.

Damon gasped and lost his focus on Jack, who kicked him away. A stake drove through his ribs from behind. They hadn't hit the heart, though, he realised dazedly, or he'd already be dead. He tried to sit up as he heard Jack get to his feet, his footsteps quickly moving away.

Siobhan stood over Damon, her blood-red lips curled in a smile. 'I wouldn't give you real poison, you fool,' she said coldly. 'I love him. No one will kill him but me.'

From behind her, came a growl of fury. Siobhan gasped, her face distorting with pain, and arched backward, her blue eyes wide and startled. Fresh red blood spread across the front of her stained white nightgown. Pulling the stake from his own back, Damon realised the tip of another stake was protruding from Siobhan's chest.

This one, though, hadn't missed the heart. Siobhan, her eyes suddenly blank, fell, her black hair spreading out around her. Behind her, with the face of an avenging angel, stood Elena.

Climbing to his feet, Damon caught Elena and pulled

her against him. Her heart was beating hard; he could feel it pounding against him.

'Are you hurt?' he asked.

Elena shook her head. 'No,' she said, sounding dazed. 'Are you all right? She staked you.'

Jack was nowhere to be seen – he must have escaped when Siobhan staked Damon. But Damon managed to arrange his face into a smile. 'It takes more than a stake to take me down, princess.' His back was aching horribly, and he could feel blood running down between his shoulder blades, soaking his shirt.

Scuffling footsteps came from behind them and Damon wheeled around to see the others coming back, supporting Matt, who leaned heavily on Alaric. Jasmine was trying to check his vitals as she hurried beside them.

'The vampires are starting to wake up,' Meredith said sharply. 'We have to go. Did the poison work?'

Damon held Elena closer. 'No.' He could feel her shock and despair resonating through the bond, echoing his own. This had been their only chance. Siobhan had lied – and they had lost their chance to take vengeance for Stefan.

Jack was gone. They were no closer to finding a way to kill him, and their one lead had turned out to be worse than useless.

They had failed.

CHAPTER

29

Bonnie clutched Matt's hand, trying to hold him steady as Jasmine steered the car around a curve. Fresh blood was staining the bandage on his neck, and Bonnie's stomach turned over. His neck had looked like a piece of raw meat.

'He's bleeding again,' she told Jasmine, her voice thin.

Jasmine's eyes flicked up to the rear-view mirror. 'Put pressure on it. We're almost there.'

Bonnie took a cloth from the seat beside her and pushed it firmly against Matt's neck. He gave a small pained grunt, a crease appearing between his eyebrows. 'Sorry, so sorry. Is this right?'

'You're doing great,' Jasmine told her.

Matt shifted, blinking his eyes open. 'M'OK,' he muttered.

'Sure you are, cowboy,' Jasmine told him. 'Just take it easy.' At the sound of her voice, Matt's face relaxed, and his eyes fluttered shut again.

Jasmine pulled the car into a spot near the front door of Elena and Damon's apartment building, and Meredith came around to the car to help Matt.

'Get the IV drip and the cooler of blood bags from the trunk, OK?' Jasmine asked Bonnie before she and Meredith hurried, supporting Matt, towards the front door, which Elena was already holding open.

Matt was in good hands, Bonnie thought, swinging open the trunk. Jasmine wasn't a fighter or magical, but she was scarily efficient. The pole for the IV was in a couple of different pieces – light, made of hollow aluminium, but awkward to carry – and Bonnie had to gather them together a couple of times before she got them tucked securely under one arm and was able to pick up the cooler with the blood bags and the tubing with the other. Everyone else had disappeared into Elena and Damon's apartment building by the time Bonnie slammed the trunk and headed inside.

Her steps faltered for a moment. When had she started thinking of it as Elena and Damon's building, not Elena and Stefan's? Sorrow shot through her, and she suddenly missed Stefan so much.

And now the man – no, the vampire – who'd killed him had gotten away. Bonnie swallowed back her tears, clutching the IV pole. They'd saved Matt. He was hurt, but they'd gotten him out of there. That was the most important thing.

Upstairs, Matt was lying on the couch, and Jasmine immediately got to work setting up the drip. 'He lost a lot of blood, but that's the worst of his injuries,' she said. 'He's going to be fine.' There were dried tear tracks on her cheeks, but her fingers were sure as they moved across the medical equipment.

'We're back to square one, aren't we?' Elena asked dismally from her chair near the couch. 'Jack and his vampires can't be killed, and he'll keep coming after us.'

'He wants Damon dead,' Meredith said flatly, 'and he wants me back at his side.'

Alaric put his arm around her, and she leaned against him, her dark head on his shoulder. 'Maybe we should cut our losses and stop hunting him,' he said hesitantly. 'It might be better to concentrate on keeping away from Jack if we don't have a chance of killing him.'

'I agree,' Jasmine said, pausing with an IV needle in her hand. 'We need to lay low. Matt could have been killed. Any of us could have.'

'We're not giving up.' Meredith said, her jaw set. Elena nodded.

There was an uneasy silence. Jasmine was glaring down at her hands as she neatly set up the IV and began to rebandage Matt's wounds. Matt moaned softly, and Bonnie saw him flinch, his eyes still firmly closed, but his lashes fluttering. He looked so vulnerable. She was used to thinking of Matt as tough, despite the fact that he was the most human of them.

Bonnie's mouth was dry with nerves suddenly, and she cleared her throat. 'I think they're right,' she said. 'We don't have anything. Like Elena said, we're back where we started. And we're the only ones in danger from him here. We don't need to protect anyone else.'

Elena and Meredith both stared at her, shocked. The three of them had always joked about their 'velociraptor sisterhood', that they always had one another's backs. Bonnie felt a wriggle of guilt, deep inside. But if there was no way forward, maybe it was time to think about retreating.

'Just because we're back to the beginning doesn't mean we quit playing,' Elena said sharply. She looked to Damon for support.

But Damon was staring into space. 'I'm not sure we have nothing.' His dark eyes narrowed as he spoke to Elena. 'Think of what Siobhan told us. She knew Jack would always make himself a back door, in case he needed to get rid of the vampires. Doesn't that sound right?'

Elena's face brightened, her irritation turning thoughtful. 'You think Siobhan was telling the truth about the poison?'

Damon arched an eyebrow at her. 'The best lies always have some basis in reality.'

'So you think there really is a poison somewhere that'll kill them?' Bonnie asked. 'Like an antidote to whatever Jack does that makes them immortal?' There was a general stirring in the room as everyone sat up straighter.

'But Siobhan's dead,' Elena said. 'Even if she knew about a real poison, we can't get the information out of her now.'

'I'll go back to Jack's laboratory in Zurich,' Damon said slowly. 'That's where I found his journal: it's where everything started. If there's a poison, he might keep it there.'

'I'm going with you,' Elena said immediately. She was leaning forward now, beginning to smile, her eyes locked on Damon's as he met her smile with one of his own. They might have been the only two people in the room.

A small motion over by the couch caught Bonnie's eye. Jasmine was holding Matt's hand between both of her own and she bent her head to kiss his knuckles. His eyes were open now, and they were gazing at each other with such a wealth of tenderness that Bonnie had to look away.

Alaric's arms were wrapped around Meredith, supporting and protecting. She sighed and cuddled against his body. He kissed the top of her head. Elena and Damon were still grinning at each other, delighted with their own cleverness.

Bonnie suddenly ached for Zander, an empty hollow ache in the middle of her chest. She remembered the cascading purple blossoms of the mimosa in Mrs Flowers's garden, the way their sweet scent had risen from her hands and clothes all the way home, filling her car with the smells of summer. Joy rising from sorrow. Second chances. It was as if she could hear Mrs Flowers whispering in her ear. Finally, Bonnie thought she understood the point of the story Mrs Flowers had told her.

No one needed Bonnie now. They were peaceful and safe, each wrapped up with the one they loved. Things were bad, there was no question about it, but they had a moment of calm now, before the storm. She slipped quietly into the hall, pulling out her phone.

Zander picked up on the first ring. 'Bon?' he asked. 'Are you all right?'

His voice sounded so good, deep and warm with that familiar rough note in it. Bonnie closed her eyes, her whole body relaxing even as tears of relief came into her eyes. She'd been trying so hard not to miss him.

She could picture him clearly, his moonlight-blond hair hanging rattily down the back of his neck – he always needed a haircut – his ocean-blue eyes quizzical and gently concerned. She could imagine that he was standing, his weight balanced evenly on the balls of his feet, ready to spring into action if she needed him. Even just if she wanted him.

'Yes,' she said. 'I'm saying yes.'

'What?' Zander sounded wary, unsure.

'Yes, I'll marry you. I'll come to Colourado. I have to help the others with the Jack situation, but we'll figure something out.' Bonnie sniffed. There was a silence on the other end of the phone. 'Zander, are you there? I love you, Zander. I was an idiot to let you go.'

'And one thing we know is that Ms Bonnie McCullough is not an idiot.' She could hear the smile in Zander's voice now.

'Damn straight,' she said.

Life was short, for humans like her, and for werewolves, too. And even if she had to leave everything here behind, she was going to marry Zander. Warmth unfurled inside her, and her eyes filled with happy tears.

She'd figure out how to keep helping her friends. But she wasn't giving up Zander. She was going to spend that life with him, no matter what. True love? True love was worth anything.

CHAPTER

30

The sign in front of the office building read lifetime solutions. Elena frowned up at it uneasily. 'That seems sort of ominous,' she said to Damon. 'Lifetime Solutions? Isn't death the only solution to a lifetime?'

It was early evening, and the flow of office workers leaving the building had slowed to a trickle. It was time to make their move.

'We all know what Jack's solution is, don't we?' Damon said. 'I still have a keycard.' He was dressed in a sleek, beautifully cut, dark suit. His idea, she supposed, of what a Swiss businessman might wear. To Elena, he looked a little too sophisticated for the role, better suited to a magazine spread than a real office. In contrast, she was wearing a skirt and blouse, an outfit she might have worn to her actual job, before Stefan had died and she'd stopped going.

She smoothed her hands over the skirt, wiping her sweaty palms, and raised an eyebrow at Damon. 'Shall we?'

They crossed the square and entered the lobby of the Lifetime Solutions building. The security guard glanced at them with interest. Elena's breath quickened. This was it. The place was probably crawling with Jack's vampires. Damon slapped the keycard against the automatic door and then, as it opened, he froze. He tried to take a step forward, then jerked to a halt again and frowned at the door.

'What's up?' Elena said, keeping her voice casual. She looked quickly at the security guard, who was looking in the other direction now.

'I can't get in,' Damon said softly. 'Jack must have done something after I stole his journal. The way's barred against me.'

Elena stepped through the door and then back out. There was nothing stopping her. 'Do you think he's got a human living in there?' she whispered.

Damon shrugged. 'Must be. It wouldn't stop the vampires he's made, only the ones like me.'

'Right. Just like sunlight or running water or stakes,' Elena agreed. The security guard was peering suspiciously at them now, and she forced a laugh. 'I can't believe you forgot it,' she said loudly and nonsensically. Damon was looking at her like she was insane, so she flicked her eyes towards the outer door. 'Let's go get it.'

'New plan,' she said, once they were outside and out of sight of the guard. 'Draw me a map of how to get to Jack's office.' They'd agreed, if he kept the poison anywhere in the building, his private office would be the most likely place. The journal had been there.

Damon tensed. He didn't like her going in alone, Elena knew. But it was the only solution. 'You'll be careful?' he asked reluctantly.

'Of course.' Elena forced a smile as she took the keycard from his hand. 'Make me that map.'

Her heels seemed to echo unnaturally loudly as she walked across the lobby a second time. But the security guard paid no attention as she used the keycard to pass through the automatic door.

Once the elevator doors had safely shut between them, Elena took a deep breath and pulled the map Damon had made out of her attaché case. Up to the fourth floor.

The elevator doors opened on to a sleek and empty reception area, all greys and whites under soft lighting. It was completely silent; there was no one in sight.

The route Damon had marked out led her past a lab full of caged rats and through a corridor lines with cubicles. She gripped her attaché case in one hand. It was partly intended for camouflage, partly so she'd have something to put the poison in if – no, when, she told herself fiercely – she found it.

She hoped it was in Jack's office, she thought, frowning through a window overlooking a laboratory full of medical equipment.

Lifetime Solutions looked just like any kind of medical research lab. She'd expected something a little more threatening, somehow.

The lights were on everywhere, fluorescent bulbs humming up above her. Even a few computers were still on, but she didn't see a single person, not until she turned the corner of the hall that led to Jack's office.

There was a man sitting at a desk outside Jack's office, a stack of papers in front of him. When Elena turned, he was clearly already expecting her, his head up and his eyes fixed on where she approached.

He must have heard her footsteps. *Human?* Elena wondered. *Vampire?* She hadn't been particularly stealthy, and the office was quiet. It was perfectly reasonable that he might have heard her, even if he lacked any special powers.

Elena tried to slow her heartbeat, to calm herself down, and kept the smile fixed on her face as she approached him. He watched her placidly, but she thought she saw an eager look cross his face for just a moment, the expression of a predator who scented prey. Was she imagining it?

As she came to a halt in front of his desk, he smiled

back up at her, a bland, professional smile. 'Kann ich der helfen, bitte?' he asked politely.

Oh no. They spoke more than one language in Switzerland, didn't they? She hadn't accounted for that in her plans. At dinner, Damon had ordered for her in French. Elena only spoke English. She could only remember a few phrases from the summer she'd spent in Paris, just enough to be sure this vampire wasn't speaking French.

'Jack sent me for some papers from his office,' she said. She kept her voice level and the smile pinned to her face. Did she look as fake as she felt? She tried to channel the persona she had used in the time she'd worked as an executive assistant: calm, polite, professional, slightly bored. 'I've come all the way from Virginia, in the United States. It's very important.'

For just a moment, something flashed through the man's aura. Something wrong, a neon red slicing through the muddy blue. *Vampire. Definitely a vampire*, Elena thought, and just managed to stop herself from taking a step backward.

The vampire's eyes sharpened at her minuscule flinch, taking on an even more predatory gleam. But when he spoke again, his voice was perfectly cordial. 'Certainly, miss. What does Dr. Daltry require?'

All of sudden, it was like something clicked into place, and her Guardian Power bloomed. A new power this time, like she was seeing inside him, watching the rhythms of the vampire's heart and mind. Elena took a quick, excited breath, her heart speeding up again.

'Listen carefully,' she told him, and there was a funny, deep echo behind her words, as if someone else, someone Powerful, was speaking in time with her. The vampire relaxed, his mouth tilting into a faint smile, and Elena could see that he wanted to obey her.

She wondered . . .

'Why don't you come with me?' she said, and the echo was still there. 'Help me look.'

With perfect readiness, the vampire rose to his feet. Elena glanced around hurriedly. She was fizzing with nervous excitement. She'd never been able to compel anyone to do what she wanted before. Would this work on everyone? Only on vampires? If her control snapped, he would kill her, she was sure. She forced herself to concentrate, holding on to her Power over him.

There. On the other side of the hall was a plain white door with a bolt. She walked over to it, the vampire following her docilely. It was a supply closet, its shelves neatly lined with envelopes of various sized pads of paper, boxes of paper clips and staples. It was like any supply closet in any office in the world, and Elena felt a funny little pang at the sight of it. It had been good, working in an office, living the daylit life with Stefan. She wouldn't ever be that girl again.

'Go in,' she told the vampire, listening to the echo of Power behind her own words. He hesitated, though, a small frown creasing his forehead. He was clearly struggling between the force of Elena's command and his natural inclinations. 'Go on,' she said, and tried to put an extra force of will behind it. She could feel him bending beneath her words, and Elena gritted her teeth and pushed.

The vampire's face smoothed out. 'Yes, Fräulein.' He stepped forward, into the closet.

'Stay,' Elena said hurriedly. 'You're fine there. You won't need anything.'

She closed the door quietly behind him and flipped the lock. She hoped the command would be enough, and that it would still work when she wasn't standing right there next to him. The lock wouldn't be strong enough to hold a vampire for long.

She rapidly crossed the hall again and went into Jack's office, shutting the door behind her. She leaned against it for a moment, taking a quick gulp of air. There was a lock, thank goodness, and she turned the latch as quietly as she could, her hands shaking.

How long did she have before this new Guardian Power's effect wore off, she wondered. Or did she have even that long? Were there security cameras watching the hall: would someone have seen her lock him in?

She firmly put it out of her mind. She needed to concentrate on the job at hand. But she had to work fast.

The office had floor-to-ceiling windows looking out

over the plaza outside, a coat closet in the corner and another door that led to a small bathroom. It looked like a normal executive office – desk, cabinets, chairs. Not too many places to hide something secret.

Damon had found Jack's journal in a secret drawer at the back of the desk, so that was the place to start. Elena seated herself in the cushy leather chair behind the desk and slid the top drawer all the way out.

On the top of the back of the drawer, just as Damon had described, was a small keyhole. Pulling the lock picks Damon had given her out of her attaché case, she slid the straight piece of metal into the lock and turned it as far as she could, then carefully inserted the long curved pick. At first, it was just like she was fishing around, rubbing a few pieces of metal together with no effect. But at her fourth try, something shifted. It took a few more tries to manage to push back all the pins inside the cylinder of the lock. Finally, though, the lock turned as neatly and easily as if she'd had the key.

'Gorgeous,' Elena breathed to herself. 'Let's see.'

Nothing. The secret compartment was empty.

Frustrated, she shoved the drawer closed again a little too hard. There was an audible clunk. Elena froze, and listened hard. There were probably other vampires in the building, and their hearing would be sharp. But there was no answering sound, and after a moment, she relaxed.

She looked hurriedly around the room. If the poison

wasn't in the secret compartment, where could it be hidden? She began to rifle through the other drawers, pulling them out and looking them over carefully. No more secret compartments, as far as she could see. No keyholes hidden in the backs of these drawers.

There was nothing in the desk, nothing fastened underneath it, either. She got to her feet and looked around. The cabinets? She froze. Had that been a noise? She drew the stake from her attaché case. If it was the vampire secretary, breaking free of her suggestion, maybe she'd be able to take him out for long enough that she could escape.

But there was no other sound. She must have imagined it. Her luck was holding, for now.

The cabinets held nothing but hanging files and, at the bottom of one, a bottle of gin.

Where else? Elena ran her hands under the cushions of the chairs, lifted the paintings on the walls and looked behind them to make sure there was no concealed safe. The closet was empty, except for a long black coat and an umbrella. Elena swung the door shut.

Wait. The memory of her favourite hiding place back home made her look in the closet again, more carefully.

There were the faintest lines across the floor. A square. Elena hurried back to the desk and found a thin bronze letter opener. She stuck it into one of the cracks and slowly prised up the panel.

Below the panel was another locked compartment.

Her hands were shaking now, and she dropped the thin pick twice before she got it in the lock properly.

Sitting at the bottom of this hidden compartment was a square box, maybe eight inches on each side, made of black metal. *Please*, Elena thought. *Please.* Carefully, she snapped back the latches and opened the box.

Inside, neatly clipped into place along the sides of the box, were six hypodermics full of shimmering blue liquid.

Elena took a moment to marvel that Siobhan had bothered to make her false poison the right colour. Perhaps she really had possessed some of the poison, although she hadn't given it to Elena and Damon. Maybe they should have searched the cave and Siobhan's cabin in the woods.

Better still, there were some papers inside the box that, based on Elena's quick glance, seemed like they might be the research notes on how Jack had developed the formula.

She sent a wave of victory, of joy, through the connection to Damon. He'd know what she meant.

As carefully as she could, hyper-aware of how fragile a syringe was, she packed the box into her case and glanced around the room. If it held other secrets, she hadn't uncovered them. And staying any longer would be pushing her luck.

Elena smoothed down her skirt and straightened her

blouse. There was one last thing she needed to do.

Leaving Jack's office, she was careful to leave the door slightly cracked, the way she'd found it. There was only silence in the hall, no sound coming from the supply closet. Her luck had held: no one seemed to have yet noticed that anything was amiss.

When she opened the supply closet, the vampire was facing the shelves of envelopes, calm and relaxed, just as she'd left him. Power thrummed through her, and she felt the tendril that held him in place, running straight from her to him. He turned to look amiably at her, awaiting her next instruction.

Elena whipped out the hypodermic she'd been holding behind her back, jammed it into the side of his throat and pushed the plunger.

The effect was instantaneous. The vampire choked, his eyes bulging. He brought his hands up to claw at his throat, pushing the empty hypodermic away. The gentle spell he had seemed to be under snapped. 'What are you doing to me?' he gasped, his voice strangled. 'What did you do?'

He fell heavily to the floor, panting. A thin stream of drool ran out across his chin. He seemed to be struggling to move, tiny twitches of his arms and legs, but he wasn't getting anywhere. His eyes, red and watering, fixed on Elena. 'Help me,' he whispered.

Elena hardened her heart. 'You would have killed me if you'd had the chance, you know you would,' she said. He only blinked, looking up at her with a dazed expression. 'Wouldn't you?' she demanded, letting a thread of the compelling echo slide into her voice.

The dying vampire twitched again. His eyes rolled back into his head. He was dead.

Steeling herself, Elena took hold of the vampire's legs and dragged him into Jack's office, where he wouldn't be found as easily. He was heavy, and his head bumped roughly against the doorframe as she pulled him through. Despite herself, Elena winced at the thump.

She pulled him over to the coat closet where the poison had been hidden and wedged him inside. Closing the closet door, she turned the latch, locking his body inside.

Combing her hair and touching up her make-up, Elena made sure that she was pristine again before she left Jack's office. It was better not to look like she had been dragging corpses around if she wanted to get out of here unquestioned. With luck, no one would look for the dead vampire until tomorrow.

She could feel Damon radiating anxiety through their bond, now that she had a moment to realise it.

She tried to send him reassurance and joy – they'd found it, they'd succeeded – but the emotions she was feeling from Damon didn't calm down. He'd be happy once she was out of Lifetime Solutions. That black box would ensure Damon's safety. Vengeance for Stefan's death.

Coming down in the elevator, Elena allowed herself for a moment to wonder if now they'd be able to move on.

No one stopped her as she crossed the lobby. Elena's heart beat faster. She was going to make it out.

Outside, it was now fully dark, and the plaza was deserted.

'Damon?' Elena called. 'I've got it.' She could sense him, somewhere nearby.

'Elena.' Jack's voice. A cold shiver ran down her back. Elena turned around.

Jack had his arm wrapped around Damon, a stake sunk halfway into Damon's chest. As she watched, he pushed the stake in a little further and a circle of bright blood began to spread across Damon's shirt. 'Elena,' Jack said again. 'I think we need to talk.'

CHAPTER
31

'The stake's touching his heart,' Jack said. 'I can kill him in a second. Give me the poison and I'll let your boyfriend go.'

Damon could hardly breathe, and with each tiny movement of the stake in Jack's hand, he felt dizzy and drained. His whole chest burned as if it were on fire. He stood as still as he could and fixed his eyes on Elena, willing her to listen to the message he was trying to send her. *Don't give it to him. Run away.*

He didn't want to die. But he couldn't live with himself if they let go of their only chance of killing Jack. Not when Jack had killed Stefan, killed Katherine.

Besides, if Elena did hand over the poison, he would probably shove the stake through Damon's heart anyway. They knew by now that they couldn't trust him.

Carefully, Damon tensed his muscles little by little, keeping himself fully aware of the stake. His best chance would be to wait for Jack to be distracted, and then to take him down quickly. Protect Elena, and perhaps even save himself. Adrenalin began to burn beneath his skin in anticipation of a fight.

'What's it going to be?' Jack said, thrusting the stake a fraction of an inch deeper. Damon flinched.

Elena didn't answer. She was standing very still, her eyes dark and huge in her pale face. She looked, Damon thought, like someone about to be burned at the stake.

'Stop this,' she said, and Damon felt a pulse of Power coming from her. Jack laughed and shook his head. Whatever Elena was trying, it wasn't working.

Damon shut his eyes for just a moment. His heart was pulsing around the stake, sending steady throbs of pain through his body. It made it hard to think.

It wouldn't be so bad to die if he had to, he supposed. He had loved. He had lived.

If only he could be sure that Jack would let Elena go.

The stake against his heart jerked, hard, and Damon's eyes flew open.

Jack yanked the stake entirely out of Damon's chest, his arm flinging wide and the stake clattering to the ground. Damon took his cue and leapt forward, ready to fight, but there was no fight to have, not right now.

Jack was being pulled backward, away from Damon,

with short, jerky steps. His arms were drawn up and suspended in mid-air, even as his body writhed, struggling. His face was twisted with rage.

Damon, his hand covering the wound on his chest, turned around to stare at Elena. As he watched, her hands came up and moved, her long elegant fingers plucking in time to the motion of Jack's limbs, puppet master to Jack's puppet. Her eyes were shining, and she looked triumphant.

'Good girl,' Damon breathed. 'Beautiful.'

He had never seen Elena use her Guardian Powers with such precision before. Elena twitched a finger and Jack's head snapped backward with an outraged snarl. He was utterly at her mercy.

Damon headed for Elena and found himself stumbling, moving at half the speed he usually could. Fresh blood was pumping out of his chest and streaming down his body as he moved. The suit would be ruined, he thought dazedly. His body was trying to knit itself together, but there was too much damage. He needed to feed.

'Use the poison,' Elena murmured as he came up to her. Her eyes were fixed unwaveringly on Jack, as if a glance aside would break her power over him.

Damon fumbled open the briefcase at her feet, unlatching the box he found inside. Five needles full of the poison, each shimmering softly in the light of the moon overhead. He grabbed one, unclipping it from the side of the box, and held it tightly but carefully as he turned back towards Jack.

Jack's eyes fixed on the hypodermic and his eyes widened. For the first time, he looked afraid.

But Elena's control was beginning to slip, Damon could see. As Damon got closer, the self-made vampire lunged towards him, grabbing desperately at the hypodermic with one hand, even as the rest of his body jerked at Elena's command.

Damon grabbed hold of the free arm, trying to force it into stillness as he raised the syringe. Maybe he could inject it here, right in the vein at the crook of the elbow.

He hesitated just for a split second, looking for the long blue line of the vein, and in that second Elena lost control. Like his puppet strings had been suddenly cut, Jack fell forward, knocking Damon to the ground. The syringe fell from his hand, skittering away across the concrete of the plaza.

Damon sucked in a breath, dazed for a moment, and Jack's fangs sunk into his throat, ripping and tearing. *Can't lose more blood*, Damon reminded himself, and struggled, shoving the other vampire away. His teeth gouged at Damon's throat as they came out, and Damon clawed viciously at Jack's face, trying to take some vengeance.

He was holding Jack away, far enough that he couldn't bite, but the other vampire's hands fumbled at his chest. They found the wound above Damon's heart and roughly, slowly, wormed their way within.

Damon gasped in shock. He could feel Jack's long fingers inside him, reaching for his heart.

Everything went grey for a moment, and when the world snapped back into colour, Damon's chest was going cold. He tried to gasp for air, but Jack was above him, blocking out the sky, his presence suffocating.

Just beside Damon, something glimmered. The syringe. Slowly, as if someone else was moving it, Damon saw his own hand slide towards it and pick it up. He fumbled for a second, and it almost fell again. And then, with new strength, he gripped the syringe and shoved it against Jack's neck.

Everything went grey. He must have lost consciousness, because when he blinked back into awareness, time seemed to have passed. Elena was pulling Jack's weight off of him and kneeling by Damon's side. Her lips were moving, but he couldn't hear what she said.

And then, with the force of a sudden slap, light and sound came back into the world.

'– please, I don't think I can take it,' Elena was saying. Damon smiled at her. It seemed to take a lot more effort than it usually did.

The ragged bite on his throat burned, and he could feel a lukewarm trickle of blood running down his side. But warmth flooded him as he looked up at Elena. She looked like an angel. 'I love you,' he said. 'Always.' It seemed so simple.

Beside them, Jack gave a rattling gasp, and Damon turned his head to look at him, the concrete cold and gritty against his cheek.

'Lucia,' Jack muttered. His eyes were wet and bloodshot. A strange, rank smell, like rotting meat, rose from him, and Damon wrinkled his nose, clutching at the wound on his own chest. 'You have to understand,' Jack said fiercely. 'Someone has to know why I did it. I loved Lucia, but Siobhan loved me. And then I found out Siobhan was a vampire.' He coughed, a loose hacking cough, and a stream of drool ran across his chin.

'And you wanted her Power for yourself,' Elena said coolly.

Jack groaned, and shook his head. 'No, it wasn't about that. Lucia got sick. All the doctors said she would die. I was half crazy . . . Siobhan came when I called her, but she wouldn't change Lucia, wouldn't fix her.'

Jack's lips twitched into a smile again, stiffer and more horrible, the rictus grin of a dying man. 'But I had another plan. I would make Siobhan save her, and I'd make myself a vampire, too. We'd live for ever, together. Strong and well.'

'Something happened, though,' Elena said. Her voice was a little warmer, Damon thought. Elena understood why someone would do terrible things for love. 'Your plan didn't work.'

Blood trickled down Jack's chin now, and he moaned and twitched as if he wanted to wipe it away but couldn't raise his hands. His eyes rolled from side to side, as if he were seeing something too horrible to look at directly. 'I found Lucia's poor body, she was torn apart . . . I was going to kill them all. I'd make more vampires, stronger, better ones, and we'd hunt down Siobhan and her kind.' He looked from Elena to Damon, his eyes pleading. 'I know . . . we're monsters. But when the vampires are dead, I'll kill my creations. It was the only way I could fight them. Let me live. Let me finish.'

His own lukewarm blood running through his fingers, Damon slowly shook his head. So what if Jack thought he was a hero? He had murdered Stefan, and he deserved to die.

Elena wrapped her arms around herself. She looked young and vulnerable, but she was Damon's strong girl. 'No,' she said. 'This is the end, Jack.'

Jack choked and gagged, a harsh cough tearing from his throat. 'Let me make the world safe,' he said weakly, when the coughing fit finally ended. 'Please. I'm not a bad man.'

He took one final rattling breath and then his chest stilled and everything was silent.

Damon took a breath of his own and stared up at the half-moon sailing high above the plaza, his chest feeling raw and painful. Jack was dead. They had their vengeance for Stefan now, and it was all over.

He had thought that it would feel better, more complete. But the flush of joy he'd felt had faded, and the ache was still inside him. Stefan was dead. He felt a slender, warm hand take his, and he turned to Elena. 'We did it,' she said softly, and Damon leaned against her. The bond between them was flooding with relief, and Damon felt his slow heart speed up a bit as he held on to Elena's hand. 'We did,' he agreed, watching the soft glow of her skin in the moonlight. 'Now we can go home.'

CHAPTER 32

Three weeks had passed since Damon and Elena killed Jack, far away in Switzerland. Since then, none of them had been able to take more than a second to focus on anything except preparing for Bonnie's wedding. And now it was a beautiful day for the ceremony, Matt thought. They were all together, safe and whole.

The sky was blue and open, the only clouds above tiny and puffy white. Birds sang in the trees – the long trill of a warbler, the three short notes of a whippoorwill. Wild violets were blooming in the grass at their feet. Matt ran a finger around the inside of his collar, easing where it pressed against the bandage on his throat.

'Dude, if you forgot the ring, Zander's going to kill you,' Spencer whispered to Jared beside him.

'Forget Zander, Shay will kill me first. She said I'd

better learn to take a little responsibility,' Jared muttered back. 'Anyway, I didn't forget it, I just can't find it.' He was digging through his pockets frantically, shaggy hair flopping over his forehead.

Matt resisted rolling his eyes. He was honoured to be the only non-werewolf in Zander's side of the wedding party. The werewolves were great guys for a pick-up game of football or a night of bar-hopping, and amazing allies in a fight. For a formal occasion? Matt felt like he'd spent the last three weeks babysitting a pack of overgrown kids. The fun bachelor party had almost made up for the nightmarish tuxedo fittings, though.

'Try the inner breast pocket of your jacket,' he whispered to Jared.

Jared felt inside his jacket and immediately smiled, a big dimpled grin. 'Thanks, Matt.'

'Loser,' Marcus whispered from his other side, and Jared snorted and smacked Marcus on the back of his head.

'Cut it out,' Matt whispered. The guys straightened up and stilled beside him as Zander came to join them, smiling nervously and shoving his pale-blond hair out of his eyes.

A Celtic harp began to play, and the gathered audience rose to their feet.

Bonnie's older sisters came down the path first, pretty and solemn-faced in rose pink. Then came Shay, Zander's second-in-command, who smirked at Jared as she stepped into place beside the sisters. Meredith followed, tall, slim and elegant, her head held high. Then Elena, her golden hair pulled back and a soft smile on her face.

The girls arranged themselves in a line in front of the minister and a hushed expectancy fell over the crowd.

They all stood and turned as Bonnie appeared, arm in arm with her beaming father. Her strapless dress was long and lacy and her red hair shone in the sunlight. She didn't wear a veil, but a circlet of white rosebuds, and she carried a bouquet of white roses in full bloom.

She looked like everything a bride was supposed to be, Matt thought: beautiful, excited, a little shy. Like a princess. Mostly, Bonnie looked happy.

She squeezed her father's arm as they came up to the others, and he kissed her, let her go and stepped back. Bonnie looked up at Zander and reached out to take his large hands in her smaller ones. He bent his head to look down at her and gave her the slow, sweet smile Matt had never seen him give to anyone but Bonnie.

Automatically, Matt glanced into the audience, looking for Jasmine, and found her seated a few rows back. Her sweet mouth curved in a private smile just for him. Something warm blossomed in Matt's chest.

He'd miss Bonnie when she went to Colourado with Zander. But love was love was love, and, basking in the light of Jasmine's sweet smile, he couldn't wish for anything else for Bonnie. This, he knew, was what was going to make his friend happy.

The minister spread his arms in greeting and the audience sat and settled. The wedding party turned their attention to him politely. Bonnie's brown-eyed gaze was confident and steady, the sunlight making her porcelain skin glow.

'Dearly beloved . . .' the minister began.

Bonnie, always the baby of their group, was now so sure and poised that a flare of affection lit in Matt's chest. He could see the skinny kid, the sassy teenager, the clear-eyed woman, all in the same person, and for a moment he was just so grateful for her, for all of them. They'd all found someone, his little band of friends: Bonnie and Zander, Meredith and Alaric – even Elena would find her way back to Damon, he knew. And he had Jasmine.

Beloved . . .

As Damon sat in the front row of seats, watching the ceremony, it occurred to him that his little redbird really had grown up. She was looking lovely, too, her face tilted politely to the minister's as she gave the appropriate responses: yes, she would have and hold, yes, she would love and honour. The overgrown werewolf boy beside her was clearly over the moon with joy, as he should be. Bonnie was too good for him.

Damon couldn't help it as his attention drifted from

little bridal Bonnie to his Elena, standing beside her. What was she thinking, his princess, behind her solemn and attentive facade? Was she wishing she and Stefan had gone through this ritual when they'd had the chance? Was she regretting all that she'd lost?

She'd loved his brother with her whole heart, and it would have been strange if she hadn't thought of that now, mourned the life they'd lost as she watched Bonnie and Zander embarking on theirs.

Or . . . could Elena be thinking of him?

He probed carefully at their bond, but got only a general contentment, a warm joy at her friend's happiness. If there was a certain wistfulness about her joy, it didn't seem to centre around anyone in particular. Not that she let Damon see, at least.

Elena had let him kiss her in the car while they hunted Siobhan. More than that, she had drawn on his energy, charged her own Power. It had been more intimate than any of their kisses before, and he still felt an echo of that closeness.

He knew what that kiss had meant to him. The question was, what had it meant to Elena? They hadn't talked about it. Since the night three weeks before when they'd killed Jack, they'd been cautious and polite with each other, circling each other warily in the confines of Elena's apartment. Every once in a while, though, he'd felt the brush of her regard, turned to see Elena's lapis lazuli eyes watching him thoughtfully and with affection.

Damon permitted himself, sometimes, to hope.

The minister said, with a smile, 'I now pronounce you husband and wife,' and Bonnie leaned up for Zander's kiss, her face shining.

Damon stood with the rest as the bridal party went down the path, and then followed and joined them as waiters passed around champagne.

Bonnie's father cleared his throat, holding his glass aloft. 'My baby girl . . .' he began, tears in his eyes. Damon let his gaze drift around the circle of faces. Bonnie's family was so ordinary – balding middle-management father, comfortably plump mother, two round-faced practical older sisters. His redbird was like a rare rose in a garden of dandelions.

'Like the cliché goes, I'm not losing a daughter, I'm gaining a son,' Bonnie's father said, putting an awkward hand on Zander's shoulder. Everyone smiled, and Damon felt a small stir of sentiment. At least they adored her, Bonnie's plebian suburban family. They'd never quite comprehend how fiery and sweet and full of Power she was. But they loved her.

When Bonnie's father finished his toast with a clumsy kiss on his daughter's cheek, Jared raised his glass. Damon hid his smile with a sip of champagne. This ought to be amusing.

'Uh . . .' the shaggy-haired werewolf began. 'When Zander started dating Bonnie, we all thought she was awesome, but we were like 'Really?' because she wasn't, uh, the same kind of person we were.' The boy paused and his eyes travelled slowly around the circle of attentive faces.

Damon could see the moment when he realised he was going to have to make this speech without using the words wolf, Pack, or Alpha. Without that, the whole lot of them were going to sound like a bunch of weirdly close-knit overgrown frat boys. Fair enough, really.

On the other side of the circle, Zander's Beta girl – Shay, that was it – twitched, and Damon could tell she was longing to smack the boy over the head.

Jared stumbled over his words, stared down at his feet, his floppy hair falling over his eyes, and finally looked up, smiling, dimples creasing his cheeks, and launched into an anecdote about Bonnie and Zander together. There was a little more alcohol in the story, Damon thought, than Bonnie's mother would have preferred, but his affection for them both shone through. Werewolf crisis averted.

Elena's arm brushed his as she stepped up next to him, and they exchanged a look of perfect understanding, amusement flowing through the bond between them.

Letting his attention wander again, Damon fingered a small rounded package in his pocket.

When the toasts were over, he pulled Bonnie aside. Zander followed amiably, a glass of champagne in his hand, and Elena stayed near them, watching. The rest of the wedding guests were drifting towards the tent set up on the other side of the meadow, where a band was warming up on the dance floor.

'Congratulations,' Damon said formally. 'I have a little something for you.' He handed Bonnie the small package, wrapped in black silk.

'But you already gave us a present,' Bonnie said, taken aback.

'I suppose so,' Damon said. Elena had ordered something from the registry from them both, he vaguely recalled – silver, perhaps, or some sort of kitchen appliance. These were the traditional gifts now, apparently. 'But this is something for you.'

Looking intrigued, Bonnie slipped the silk away from her present. A glossy white stone shone in her hand, half the size of her palm, with glistening highlights of green and blue. In its top was deeply etched a rough representation of a wolf's face.

'A moonstone,' Bonnie said, examining it. 'They're supposed to help keep the bond between lovers strong.' She looked touched, her eyes soft, as she ran her finger across the carving.

'It seemed appropriate. This particular one is quite old. I got it from an acquaintance in Zurich. Legend says that it gives its owner power over werewolves.' Damon couldn't resist shooting a sly smile at Zander, but the wolf-boy only laughed.

'She's got plenty of power over me already,' he said, and squeezed Bonnie's hand.

'Oh, Damon,' Bonnie said, and, letting go of Zander, flung her arms around Damon's neck.

Damon kissed her gently on the top of her head. Her red curls smelled as sweet as cherry candy. He hoped she'd be very happy.

'Behave yourself, wolf,' he said sternly, looking at Zander over Bonnie's head. Zander tilted his head up in acknowledgment, his face open and guileless.

Elena came closer, and Damon let Bonnie go.

'Come on then, princess,' he said, holding out his hand to Elena. He nodded towards the dance floor, where the musicians had begun to play. 'Let's dance.'

Her arms around Alaric's neck, Meredith swayed with him in time to the slow, romantic song. The cake had just been cut, Bonnie and Zander feeding each other as they laughed, a smudge of icing high on Zander's cheek. The dance floor was emptier than it had been all night. Most of the guests were laughing and chattering as they ate. But Meredith didn't want to be with everyone else, not even Elena, or Bonnie's family, who she'd known for most of her life. Not now.

'Remember our wedding?' Alaric said softly, his hand firm against her back. Meredith nodded against Alaric's shoulder. Theirs had been more formal, two hundred guests in a church instead of fifty in a meadow, but she had been as happy as Bonnie's glowing face was right now.

'Bonnie caught my bouquet,' she remembered.

'Well, I guess that worked out, then.' Alaric grinned. He led her into a long, lazy twirl. 'I hope they're as happy as we are.'

She could smell their blood, all these guests, mixed in with the smells of hair gel and icing sugar. She'd need to go out to the woods and feed later tonight.

Alaric smoothed his hand down her back. He must have felt her stiffen. 'You're not a monster.' His heart beat steadily, a comforting sound. She pulled back a little and looked at him. Alaric's skin was the golden tan he turned in the summer, darker freckles scattered across the bridge of his nose. He looked at her with total confidence, his brown eyes warm and trusting. 'You choose not to be a monster.'

He believed everything he said, Meredith knew. He was sure she wouldn't fall, sure she could resist the call of human blood, keep her humanity. She sighed and laid her head on his shoulder again.

'I'll probably be like this for ever,' she said. They'd found a poison to kill Jack, but in all his notes, there still hadn't been any mention of a cure.

'We'll find a way to fix this,' Alaric said, moving steadily in time to the music. 'But even if we don't, I'm still in. Till death do us part.'

Meredith laughed, a dry, almost painful laugh. 'You're the one who's keeping me human. You think I'm so strong, but it's all you.'

It was true, she thought, truer than Alaric would ever believe.

'When we cut the cake,' Alaric said. 'And you fed me a piece, I looked at you, and I thought, *Here. This is where I want to be for ever.*'

'I know,' Meredith said.

All she wanted was a human life with Alaric. Their little apartment, studying and talking, those discussions on any topic under the sun that fired them up and kept them debating late into the night. She wanted to wake up next to him and eat breakfast together, come home and kiss him hello and make dinner, go to bed together. Go on vacations. Have children. Grow older. Every day for the rest of their lives.

'I don't want you to drink it,' she said suddenly to Alaric, and felt him tense in her arms. He knew what she was talking about. That bottle of shining effervescence, the water of Eternal Life and Youth.

She tried to put all the aching love she felt for him, for the normal human life they should have together, that sometimes felt so far out of reach. 'I don't want you to live for ever. I don't want either of us to. Till death do us part, like you said. That's the way it's supposed to be.'

Alaric ran his fingers lightly over her cheek, kissed

her once, twice, soft brushes of his lips. 'We're going to find a cure,' he said, pulling her closer. 'I promise.'

Bonnie kicked off her high-heeled shoes to walk in the wet grass of the meadow, hand in hand with Zander, her dearest friends around her. Elena and Damon, Meredith and Alaric, Matt and Jasmine, walking together, happy and tired. Shay, who had caught the bouquet, trailed behind, holding hands with Jared.

It was getting late, and the stars were shining brightly overhead.

'This has been the best wedding ever,' she said.

'Totally unbiased opinion there,' Matt said behind her, and everyone laughed.

Everyone she loved most had come to Bonnie's wedding. When they'd slipped out of the tent, Mrs Flowers had been deep in conversation with friendly, freckled Alysia, who'd worked with Bonnie to help her reach her full magical potential. Bonnie's older sisters, Mary and Nora, shared a slice of cake at the same table, Bonnie's baby nephew peacefully asleep in Nora's lap.

The whole Pack had been there, and the High Wolf Council had come to give Zander their blessing. Rick, Marilise and Poppy, whom Bonnie had practised magic with in Chicago, had come. Friends of both Bonnie and Zander's from college whom they hadn't seen for ages. Sue Carson from high school. Bonnie's parents had danced to Motown, and her Scottish grandmother had read Bonnie's palm, promising her a long and happy married life.

Almost everyone she loved. Her heart ached a little for Stefan, who should have been with them, but she knew he would have rejoiced for her, too.

'We got married,' she told Zander, her voice full of awe.

'I know,' he said solemnly. 'Crazy, huh?'

'Do you feel any different, Bonnie?' Elena asked, amused.

'Sort of,' Bonnie said, tipping her head back to look up at the stars. Her hair had come mostly out of its French braid and long strands tickled her shoulders. 'Happier.'

'Me too,' Zander said softly.

There was a magnolia tree near them, its heavy waxy white blossoms hanging overhead, filling the air with their sweet, heady scent. Bonnie considered the tree for a moment. She reached for the Power inherent in the earth, wiggling her toes into the cold damp grass, feeling the soil beneath.

Every kind of life was connected. Everything in the universe had its own Power. If there was one truth Bonnie had learned, it was that. Cupping her hands into the shape of a magnolia blossom, she curled her toes against the soil, thought of the distant stars, and lifted.

On the tree branch above, a magnolia blossom slowly began to fill with light. Another one lit, and then another, until the whole tree was gently glowing. Alaric let out a low sound of appreciation.

Bonnie flicked a finger, and a blossom detached itself from the tree. Borne up as if on a breeze, it floated gently into the sky. Another followed, then more, until a trail of glowing blossoms, like little lanterns, floated up above the trees. They hovered and dispersed, sailing off in all directions.

'Wow,' Matt said. Bonnie looked at him, looked at them all, their faces upturned and gently lit by the glowing blossoms and the stars.

'I'm going to miss you guys,' she said softly. But she smiled. Zander's arms went around her waist and he gently kissed her cheek.

It was all going to work out. No matter where Bonnie went, no matter what new danger threatened, she and her friends would never lose each other. Somehow, in that moment, Bonnie was sure of it.

CHAPTER

23

Still in her bridesmaid's gown, Elena turned on to Maple Street and stopped the car in front of her childhood home. Her house, she reminded herself. Stefan had bought it for her.

Stefan. She curled into herself for a moment, pressing her forehead against the cool window as she looked at the house.

She had always intended to marry Stefan. She had felt like she was already married to him really, bonded together in all the ways that mattered. But she'd wanted the celebration, too. She'd thought about it idly: herself in an elegantly simple, flowing gown, her baby sister Margaret in the periwinkle-blue that brought out her eyes. Stefan, handsome and strong, his often melancholy eyes glowing with joy.

She'd counted on that wedding. But when you knew you had for ever, there wasn't a lot of impetus to do everything right away.

Then Stefan had died, and for ever was over.

Elena straightened up and wiped at her eyes with both hands. They'd gotten their vengeance, she and Damon. They killed Stefan's murderer. Jack had died in terrible pain, and at their hands.

It didn't make any difference, though, not to the way Elena felt. They'd come home from Zurich, and the wound left by Stefan's death was still raw inside her, a constant gnawing ache. After they'd killed Jack, she'd expected to feel better, to feel like she'd given Stefan something. But it hadn't helped.

She'd never gotten to say goodbye to Stefan. Bonnie had tried so hard, but they hadn't been able to find him.

And today, standing with the bridesmaids at Bonnie's wedding, listening to the minister, she'd suddenly been flooded with thoughts of Damon. Damon, who'd looked up at her from the ground in that Swiss courtyard, blood streaming from his wounds, and told her he loved her. Damon, with whom she'd always had a special bond, even before the Guardians had made it literal. Gorgeous, sardonic, clever Damon.

Stefan's brother.

She couldn't love him back. Not the way he wanted her to, the way that maybe she wanted to, as well. Not while Stefan was still waiting for her, somewhere out of reach.

She sat perfectly still in the driver's seat for a minute, just staring at the house where she'd grown up.

When she thought of home, her true home, it wasn't the apartment she and Stefan had lived in together, where Damon now slept on the couch. It was here, the house she'd lived in for the first part of her life, until after the Salvatore brothers had come to Fell's Church and everything had changed.

When this is over, we're going to go everywhere, she remembered Stefan saying. *I'll show you all the places I've been, and we'll find new parts of the world together. But we'll have your house, the place you grew up in, to come home to. We'll have a home together.*

She had cried then, full of joy and tenderness, and now her eyes filled with tears again. It was all such a waste.

They'd never had a chance to come here together, not as the house's owners. She didn't know if she was going to keep the house now, or sell it. Maybe she would lock it up and leave it just the way it was. Let it be drowned in cobwebs, like Miss Havisham's wedding cake.

But she had needed to come here once. It would be, somehow, rude and wrong to not accept Stefan's last gift.

Damon had offered to come with her. But she

couldn't bring him on her first visit to the home Stefan had bought for them both. This was something she had to do alone.

If she was ever going to move forward, she had to face the future she and Stefan would have had together. She had to let it go.

Elena got out of the car and walked quickly across the lawn, her heels leaving little holes in the grass. She passed the big quince tree, and climbed the steps to the front porch.

The key turned in the lock, but when Elena flicked the light switch, nothing happened. Of course, the electricity must have been turned off. It had been months. That would be the first thing she'd have to get settled.

Pausing for a moment, she realised that she had decided: this was her house. She was keeping it.

Aunt Judith, Robert and Margaret had taken the furniture with them to their new apartment in Richmond, but there was a candle on the window ledge by the front door.

She lit the candle with the matches she found beside it and tucked the matches into the tiny purse, matching her bridesmaid's dress, which she carried over one shoulder.

The flickering flame of the candle sent shadows sliding wildly across the walls. Climbing the stairs, Elena automatically skipped over the squeaky fifth step. She remembered skipping the same step when she had snuck out at night to cruise the quiet, darkened streets of Fell's Church in Meredith's car, when they were high school juniors.

She could still see the unfaded patches of wallpaper where picture frames had hung. She could imagine each in her mind's eye: her parents, Margaret as a baby, prom, Aunt Judith and Robert's wedding, Stefan and Elena, their arms around each other.

Her heart ached. They should have come here together.

At the end of the upstairs hall was the door to her old bedroom. Part of Elena didn't even want to go in. She remembered lying there with Stefan, how he would speed away when Aunt Judith approached so she wouldn't get into trouble. It had been a more innocent time.

There were also the windows she'd peered out every morning, where she'd seen Stefan striding across the lawn. The secret space beneath her closet floor where she had hidden her diary. A hundred slumber parties, when she and Meredith and Bonnie, and Caroline, who had been her friend then, had giggled and shared secrets, a score of evenings before high school dances when they'd done their make-up together and talked about boys.

Memories of Damon landing on her bedroom window as a crow, more than once. He'd laid beside her on the bed, after escaping the Dark Dimension, when she'd been so happy just to realise that he was still alive.

Ready for a flood of memories, Elena turned the knob and went inside.

'Elena,' the voice was soft but unmistakable, full of love and longing.

'Stefan,' she said, and dropped the candle. The flame went out and left her in total darkness.

Strong arms circled her and Elena let herself fall into them. She was surrounded by the familiar smell that meant Stefan – something green and growing, and just a touch of exotic spice. Tears ran down her cheeks. 'Stefan,' she sobbed, and buried her head in his shoulder, wrapping her arms around him. He was shaking, crying, too, a gentle hand running through her hair.

'You're not really here,' she whispered, clutching his strong, well-remembered arms, reaching up to touch his face.

And even though she had just been thinking about how Damon had been dead and returned and come back to her alive again, she knew that what she said was true. Stefan was solid in her arms, but no matter how hard she clutched at him, something in her, something she could feel was true told her: *No. not yours. not any more.*

Stefan let out a long breath, and he held her tightly against him for one more moment, and then he let her go. 'No,' he said softly, sorrowfully. 'I'm only visiting, and we don't have long.'

Elena knelt and felt around on the floor for the candle. When her hands finally closed around it, she stood and dug the matches out of her purse to relight the flame.

When the candle was lit once more, she could see Stefan. He was there, watching her with his leaf-green eyes. She'd never thought she'd see them again.

'We tried,' she said, gasping. It seemed important that he know this. 'Bonnie and I, we tried to reach you. And you weren't anywhere. Do you mean to tell me that all I had to do was come here?'

Stefan had been watching her gravely, his eyes sad, his perfect mouth with its little sensual curve turned down. 'I guess so,' he said. 'Or rather, when you were ready to come here, I could, too.'

Not wasting another moment, Elena stepped forward and caught him in a kiss. 'I've missed you so much,' she said, half laughing, half crying against his lips. 'This – to see that you're OK, that you're not just . . . gone.'

Stefan pressed his lips against hers and Elena fell into the kiss, feeling his love and longing, the sorrow he felt at having left her and the joy that she had survived, that she was turning her face back towards the sun, finding pleasure in life again.

When they broke the kiss, he held her close. 'I'm all right,' he said. 'I've gone on, but it's OK. I'll always love you.' Elena gave a half-sob, reaching up to stroke his cheek, touch his hair, reassure herself that he was there.

Stefan caught her hand and kissed it. 'Listen, Elena,' he said softly. 'I don't want you to stop because of me. You're going to live for ever, Elena, you have to live. You can't pretend I'm coming back.'

Elena opened her mouth to speak, but Stefan shook his head. 'If it's Damon . . . We were all tangled up when I was alive, but now . . .' He shrugged. 'He's always understood parts of you that I didn't, and he loves like he does everything else. With all he has.'

Elena shook her head. It felt wrong to think about this, talk about this, with Stefan in her arms. 'I want you,' she said. 'I didn't stop loving you. I won't.'

Stefan pulled her closer, dropped a kiss on the crown of her head. 'You don't have to. But you don't have to mourn me for ever, either.'

He was already fading. She tried to hold on to him, but it was like holding on to a shadow. He lowered his mouth and kissed her one last time, sweet but barely there. 'It's up to you,' he told her. 'But know I'm all right. And tell Damon I'm sorry for all the bad blood between us. We were brothers again, by the end.'

'I will, Stefan, I will.' Elena was sobbing freely, trying to hold on to Stefan as his image wavered, his voice getting softer.

'Live well, Elena. I'll always love you.'

And then Stefan was gone.

Three hours later, Elena was back in Dalcrest. Dawn was breaking and sleepy birds began chirping to each other in the trees as she let herself into the apartment.

Damon was standing by the windows in the living room, waiting for her. She stopped and stared at him, struck anew by how beautiful he was – fine boned and sleekly arrogant – and how different from classically profiled, noble-faced Stefan.

'Are you OK?' he asked. Elena realised she must look a mess, her gown stained with the dust of the uninhabited house, her eyes wild, her hair dishevelled, her face streaked with tears.

'I've always loved you,' she said. 'I won't ever stop loving Stefan, but that doesn't mean my feelings for you are any less.'

For a moment, Damon's eyes shone and a soft smile broke over his face.

But then he hesitated, and his gaze clouded over. Stefan. Like a shout, the word hung in the air between them. Elena knew that, somehow, loving her felt like more of a betrayal to him than it ever had when Stefan was alive.

'I saw Stefan,' she said. 'Stefan's ghost. He was in my house in Fell's Church. He couldn't stay long, but he was there.'

Damon sucked in a startled breath. For a moment, his expression was full of wonder and alarm, and then it went smooth and perfectly blank, the way it always did when Damon was concealing strong emotion.

'No,' Elena said sharply, and took a quick step across the living room to grab hold of Damon's arm. 'No, he was fine. He seemed . . . content. He wants us to be happy. He wants me to keep living, to go after what I want.' She tried to smile at Damon, although her face felt stiff and strange. 'He had a message he wanted me to give you.'

Damon's face softened. For a moment, he looked young, like the boy he'd been, who'd died on his brother's sword so long ago. 'He did?' he asked.

Elena nodded. 'He said he was sorry about all the bad blood there'd been between you, and he wanted me to tell you that you were brothers again, by the end.'

Ducking his head, Damon smiled, a small, private smile that Elena had never seen before. And then he wiped that smile from his face, replacing it with his customary brilliant flash of teeth. 'Well, I knew that, of course,' he said. 'Just like Stefan, to show up as a ghost and state the obvious.'

Elena took his hand and tugged him towards the couch, coaxing him to sit beside her. 'I guess I should have known what he told me, too.'

Damon went very still. 'What did he tell you?'

Running her fingers across the back of his hand, tracing the long bones of his fingers, Elena said slowly,

'He told me that, if what I wanted was . . . you . . . if I loved you . . . he'd be happy for me.'

Damon was staring very hard at the opposite wall, his dark eyes unreadable. 'And is it?' he asked, sounding almost indifferent. 'Am I what you want?'

'Oh, Damon, you know I've always loved you,' Elena said, her voice breaking. 'Even when I wasn't supposed to.'

Damon turned to her then, a new light dawning in his eyes, his mask of indifference breaking and letting hope shine through. Elena leaned towards him, sorrow and joy mixing together inside her, and their lips met.

His kiss was as soft as silk, but somehow demanding, too, and Elena opened to it. Between them, their bond flooded with emotion: love and joy, a sweet thrill of acceptance at last.

Yes, she thought, the joy conquering the sorrow just as, outside, the sun broke over the horizon. *Yes. This is my future.*

CHAPTER

34

'But the Eiffel Tower closes at eleven, it says so right on the sign,' Elena objected, laughing. 'If you didn't compel anyone, how did you get us up here so late?'

'As well as being incredibly charming and handsome, I am also extremely wealthy,' Damon told her dryly. 'Any human could have spread a few euros around. You said you wanted to come up here.'

'I'm not complaining,' Elena told him. She leaned against the railing of the observation deck, taking in the lights of Paris below them. Damon grinned at her.

'I was here in Paris when it was being built for the Exposition Universelle, you know,' he said. 'Hideous. Completely ruined the skyline. A bunch of artists drew up a petition against it. They called the Tower a useless monstrosity, and a truly tragic street lamp.'

'Oh, you're just teasing me,' Elena said, swatting at him.

'It's true,' Damon said. 'They said it in French, of course. Ce lampadaire véritablement tragique.'

Elena snorted and turned back to gaze over the city. Damon leaned beside her.

'It is rather pretty up here, of course,' he said. 'It's one of the few spots in Paris from which you can't see the Eiffel Tower.'

Despite herself, Elena giggled, and Damon laughed along with her. The golden lights of the city below reflected in her lapis lazuli blue eyes. She was so eager to take everything in, to get all the pleasure Paris had to give her.

Damon looked out over the skyline. His eyes caught on the Arc de Triomphe. Elena would probably like to see that up close, too. He was going to show her the whole world.

A jarring wave of pain came through their bond and Damon flinched. Beside him, Elena suddenly gagged and doubled over.

'Are you all right?' Damon asked, steadying her.

Elena shook her head, her face paper-white. She was clutching her stomach, her arms tightly wrapped around herself. The pain, which Damon had instinctively dampened, was still flowing through the bond. Elena was in agony.

'Sit down,' Damon said, guiding her to a bench.

Elena started gasping for breath. Doctor, he thought. Hospitals. Appendicitis? It would be faster to take her in his arms and run than to call an ambulance. Everything was in sharp focus, his mind speeding. 'We need to get you down,' he said, keeping his voice calm.

From behind them came the sound of a quiet step, and Damon whipped around. He had been sure they were alone.

The step belonged to a blonde woman, or something that chose to look like a woman. She was neatly dressed in a navy-blue suit and perfectly coiffed. Her face was stern and, as she met Damon's eyes, her own were cold. The Guardian who had bound them together. Mylea.

Something in him hardened into suspicion and then into certainty. He lunged for her, but his hand stopped, suspended in air, a few inches from her.

Her voice was as cold as ice. 'Damon Salvatore,' she said formally. 'We find you in violation of your oath. As you murdered Henrik Goetsch, also called Jack Daltry, in Zurich, Elena Gilbert's life is now forfeit.'

Elena made a choking sound and Damon grabbed her hand. 'Wait,' he said, as Mylea began to turn away. The Guardian stopped and looked at him. 'Jack was a vampire,' he said. 'He wasn't a human. He wasn't covered by my oath.'

Mylea gave a click of her tongue, as if irritated by some minor error. 'Henrik Goetsch chose to turn himself into a monstrosity. He was a human who imitated the traits of a vampire, but he never died. His human life did not end until you murdered him.'

Elena choked again, her free hand pawing at her throat. Her nose began to bleed, a thin red trickle.

'No,' Damon said, his voice raising frantically. 'He was a vampire. We didn't know . . .'

Mylea arched an eyebrow. 'There are no loopholes in the law of the Guardians.' And with that, she turned on her heel, took one step forward and was gone, blinked into nothingness.

Elena moaned and slid off the bench, on to the ground. Dropping to his knees beside her, Damon pulled her close. The blood was flowing faster, smearing across her lips and chin.

'It's all right, princess,' Damon said, stroking her hair, trying to ease Elena's suffering. 'I won't let them have you. We'll do whatever it takes.'

His mind began to buzz with rage. He wasn't going to let Elena die, not because of him. No matter what he had to do, he was going to save her.

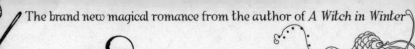
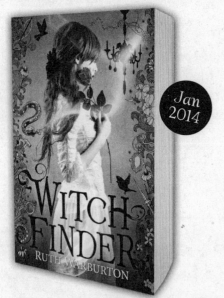